THE DIFFERENCE
BETWEEN
WOMEN AND MEN

THE DIFFERENCE

BETWEEN

WOMEN AND MEN

Stories

BRET LOTT

Random House   New York

Copyright © 2005 by Bret Lott

Published in the United States by Random House, an imprint
of The Random House Publishing Group, a division of
Random House, Inc., New York.

RANDOM HOUSE and colophon are registered trademarks of
Random House, Inc.

Original publication information for the previously
published stories that appear in this collection
can be found beginning on page 187.

Library of Congress Cataloging-in-Publication Data
Lott, Bret.
The difference between women and men: stories / Bret Lott.
p.   cm.
ISBN 0-375-50262-9
1. United States—Social life and customs—Fiction. I. Title.
PS3562.O784D54 2005
813'.54—dc22   2004058442

Printed in the United States of America on acid-free paper

www.atrandom.com

2 4 6 8 9 7 5 3 1

First Edition

Book design by Simon M. Sullivan

Title page photograph © CORBIS

This book is for

Joe De Salvo

and

Rosemary James

"The days are coming," declares the Sovereign Lord,
    "when I will send a famine through the land—
not a famine of food or a thirst for water,
    but a famine of hearing the words of the Lord.
Men will stagger from sea to sea
    and wander from north to east,
searching for the word of the Lord,
    but they will not find it."

—Amos 8:11–12

Contents

FAMILY

IN THE HEAT OF THE FIGHT, THEY FORGOT ABOUT THE CHILDREN.

They were yelling at each other about an issue neither could now recall. They could only remember that one or the other of them had been wronged somehow.

Then she'd stopped, said, "Where are the kids?"

"Of course," he shouted, "it would be you to take the higher ground. It would be you to bring the kids into this, make me feel like a heel for not thinking about them!"

"And of course," she shouted, "it would be you to think I'd use them as a weapon against you!"

But then they fell silent, and the quiet of the moment—neither could now recall when there had been silence in the house—infused them both with fear, so that they dropped their hands from the authoritative gestures they'd held them in, index finger of one hand pointed at the other's face, the other hand clenched in a fist at the hip, and let their arms go loose, useless.

They had forgotten about the children.

"Where are they?" he said, but she was already out of the room, headed upstairs.

She could not find them in their rooms, saw only evidence they had been here before: In Scott's room were plastic models of fighter jets hung by fish line from the ceiling; on the walls were pennants of major league baseball teams and posters of heavy metal bands with names such as The Broken Necks and The Disease. The dresser in Jennifer's room was strewn with barrettes and combs, the bed left unmade and littered with Barbies and teen magazines, at least a dozen different outfits heaped on the floor inside the closet.

But the children were not there.

He checked the garage, saw their bicycles, Jennifer's with the wicker basket, the purple streamers off the ends of the handlebars, Scott's with the black banana seat and chrome sissy bar. There was more in there, too, to suggest to him the lives of his children: a half-deflated basketball, a pair of skis leaned against the wall beside the shovel and rake and hoe, a pink plastic Barbie Dream House, perched atop it a plastic jeep, a couple of Scott's G.I. Joes in the front seat.

But there was only evidence of the children here. Not the children themselves.

This was when he remembered the swimming pool out back, stretched over it a green tarp littered with leaves. He feared the worst: his two children climbing under the tarp, then drowning in some freak accident like those he read about routinely in the morning paper. The pool itself had been covered, as best he could recall, since a week or so after Labor Day, when the air had turned cold perhaps a little too early and the leaves had started to change, and as he made his way through the living room to the sliding glass windows onto the back patio, he pushed aside the image in him of his two drowned children and let fill him instead that old joy of raking leaves into piles and then burning them with Scott, the two of them armed with rakes and standing still and quiet before the smoldering heaps, the rich and deep aroma of burning leaves a smell like no other, and he remembered then how he cherished this time with his son, fall's leaves a tangible truth that we all grow old, that winter is fast upon each of us, but that, too, spring will come again, and the trees will burst wholly green with proof positive of life's renewal. Father and son, he thought.

He moved out onto the deck, looked at the pool, the empty trees, the small shed huddled out among them, that place where he kept the pool cleaning equipment and various other summer items: beach chairs, the barbecue, an ice chest.

But it was the pool he was headed for, the pool and what horrors it might hold for him at this very moment.

Then he was at the edge and he knelt, lifted a corner of the tarp, fearful of what he might find there.

He saw nothing, the water opaque and dark, no light other than the sliver he'd let in with pulling back the corner of the tarp.

He stood, pulled back more of it, the tarp heavy and ungainly, and he felt his heart pounding for the work of it; felt, too, the way his muscles seemed suddenly his enemy, unable and unwilling to exert the force needed to do this work.

He managed the tarp halfway across the pool, walked the huge sheet of green plastic away from the deep end, until he knew there was enough light to see the entire length and depth of the pool, still in him this fear of what he would find there.

But there were no children in the pool. He took in a breath,

thankful for the twisted blessing this was: His children were not
at the bottom of the pool, yet still they were missing.

He looked up at the trees, at the bare branches up there, and
longed for his children, in him the melancholy of autumn, the
smell of burning leaves and the image of Scott and himself staring into smoke like some dream he might have had years before,
back when his heart was strong, his arms willing and able to
work.

But where were the children? he wondered, and let go the
tarp, turned to the storage shed.

She turned from the bedrooms, headed down the hall toward
the bathroom in the vague hope they might be there, Scott
maybe combing his hair for school, Jennifer doing her best to
French-braid hers all by herself. It was then she remembered
her promise to her daughter last night as she'd tucked the girl
into bed, that promise to French-braid her hair for school this
morning.

She thought of those moments at the close of a day when she
sat on the edge of her daughter's bed, Jennifer lying on her side
and facing the open bedroom door. The bedroom light off, it
was then she listened to the girl's cares and woes, listened and
saw in her daughter's eyes the glint and sparkle of light from the
hall, Jennifer's words a song of life, whether she spoke about the
boy she liked, David Burgess, and how he'd drawn with a pen a
devil's pitchfork on her sneaker during naptime; or spoke of
how her best friend, Lisa Spuhler, had beaten her at tetherball
on the playground; even as she spoke of her brother, Scott, and

how he'd let the air out of her bike tires just to be mean, and how much she hated him.

They were words of a child's sorrow and joy, and as she listened each night she gently touched at her daughter's auburn tresses, carefully lifted long tendrils of it away from the girl's face, laid them behind her head and across the pillow, her daughter's hair then a swirling and perfect wave, beautiful hair, hair the same color as her own, hair just like her own when she was her daughter's age, the color and length and beautiful sheen of it evidence sure enough of the passing of blood between generations, the beautiful gift of life: *Mother and daughter,* she thought.

She reached for the bathroom door, hoped to see inside two children preparing for school, and she resolved in the moment she pushed open the door that she would take care of her daughter's hair for her, would even drive her in to school if they were late as a result of the braiding.

But they were not there.

The bathroom was empty, inside only the *101 Dalmatians* shower curtain crowded with cartoon puppies, dinosaur and Care Bear bath towels on the racks, the sink counter strewn with even more of Jennifer's barrettes and clip combs, Scott's single black plastic pocket comb.

Only an empty children's bathroom, and in spite of her fears she smiled at the familiarity of it, the welcome sight of the room, all this evidence of their children's lives.

But where, she still worried, were the children?

"Found them!" she heard then, her husband calling from outside, his voice reaching her through the small window above the bathtub. "They're out here!" he shouted.

She felt her heart ease, the melancholy of the missed moments of her hands moving deftly in her daughter's hair gone now with the good knowledge Jennifer hadn't yet left for school. She could still braid her hair.

And what were they doing outside? she thought, as she made her way back to the kitchen, then to the living room, where the sliding glass window stood open to reveal to her a sharp fall morning, bare trees, the swimming pool cover peeled back, the surface of the water already scattered with leaves.

It was then he emerged from the storage shed, smiling, a proud look on his face, and for a moment she believed he'd use this triumph of his against her once the fight picked up again.

She saw, too, he had the little Igloo cooler they used to take with them to football games and on day trips, the small one that held only a few sodas, a couple of sandwiches. He carried it not by the handle but with the cooler set atop his hands like a pillow bearing a crown. Or the body, she thought for a moment, of a dead child borne from the depths of the pool. But it was only an ice chest, she thought, and a little one at that, and she felt a brief smile play across her face, felt herself blink.

He held the cooler with both hands, careful not to tip it or drop it for what he'd found inside it, and now he stepped out of the shed and into light down through empty trees, light so sharp and cutting it seemed to slice into him, a sky too bright and sharp for words.

She walked around the edge of the pool, came toward him,

and he saw how she looked past him, toward the doorway into the shed, as though there might be something inside he'd over-looked.

She stood before him, and he saw her eyes go from the cooler to his own eyes to the cooler again.

She said, "So where are they?"

"Where do you think?" he said, and nodded at the cooler. Still he smiled at her.

He knelt, still just as careful with the cooler as he'd been since he'd taken it from the top shelf, drawn there by a strange and muffled sound, a rhythm of some sort that seemed to have emanated from the cooler, next to it on one side the dust-covered Coleman lantern, on the other a rusted and label-less can of paint.

He looked at his wife one more long moment and saw in her features the same fear he'd known until a few moments ago.

He pulled open the lid, just as she leaned over, hands on her knees, her eyes darting from him to the cooler and back again, not certain what might happen next.

Then the lid was away, the handle pulled back, and she saw them: their children, there in the cooler. Two small people no bigger than Jennifer's Barbies, Scott's G.I. Joes.

But they weren't children, she could see; they were adults. There was Scott, his black hair cut short and with a neatly trimmed beard. He was sitting in a recliner, footrest up, there in the cooler. He had on a blue button-down shirt and khaki slacks and leather slippers; across from him, against the wall of the cooler, sat a color television set. Scott held an arm out in front of him; in his hand, she could see a television remote control. He clicked through the stations, tiny pictures skimming across the screen too fast to make sense.

Next to him was Jennifer, her hair short and in a stack perm. She had on a tiger-striped leotard, purple tights, and seemed to be skipping in place, her feet doing a little dance, her arms moving up and down. Before her was a television of her own, playing on the screen a minuscule woman dressed much like Jennifer and doing the same moves: an aerobics video, she realized.

All this inside the little cooler.

She felt tears well up at the joy of finding them, and touched at her eyes.

She glanced at her husband, whispered, "That was close."

"No kidding," he whispered back. "But I don't remember them being this—this old."

He stole a glance at his wife, who seemed suddenly much older as well.

She whispered, "And I don't remember them being this—this small." She stole a glance at her husband, who seemed no smaller now than when they'd been fighting only a few minutes before.

"At least I found them," he said. "You don't have to criticize me for how big they are."

"I'm not," she said. "That's not what I meant at all. It's just like you to think anything I say is an attack on you."

"Just don't start up," Scott said then, and they both looked at him, still with his hand out, the remote pointed at the television.

No one said anything. There were only the smallest of sounds coming from the two televisions: the jumbled array of words and music from the programs Scott sped through, and the rhythmic bump of dance music from Jennifer's video, the instructor's chirped exhortations: *Go for the burn! You can do it!*

"Thank you," Jennifer said. She dropped to the floor, lay on her right side, and started leg lifts in time with the music.

After a moment, the father said, "For what?"

"For not starting up, what do you think?" Scott said. Still he hadn't looked at them, only stared at the television: his son, leaned back in the recliner, feet up.

"Careful how you talk to your father," the mother said.

Scott shrugged, still looked at the set.

She forced a smile, said, "So, Jennifer, when did you cut your hair?" She tried to make the words sound easy and informal, as though they hadn't lost the children, and as though they hadn't grown old and small and been found in a cooler in the shed.

"What do you mean—" Jennifer began, then sat up, quickly moved onto her left side, started doing leg lifts again "—cut my hair?"

"You know," she said, and touched at her own, that auburn-gone-gray. "Your hair." She paused. "You used to wear it so— so long and beautiful."

"I wore it in a pixie my whole life, Mother," Jennifer said. Now she moved onto her tummy, lifted one leg and then the other behind her, just as did the perky woman on the television. "I had it permed awhile ago."

"I'm trying to watch the television here," Scott said.

"But," the mother said. "But you wanted me to French-braid it just last night. Just last night when I tucked you in."

"Must have been somebody else," Jennifer said. "Sorry to burst your bubble."

The father said, "You watch how you talk to your mother, little girl," then looked at his wife.

"But her hair," his wife said to him. "I used to braid it—"

"I don't know what a pixie is," her husband said to her, "but she sure as heck never wore it long enough for braids."

"I said I'm trying to watch the television," Scott said, even louder now. "Hello out there," he said. Still he hadn't moved.

"Maybe you need to get your butt up out of that chair," his father said, and glanced at his wife, winked at her. He smiled, the wink and his smile intended as a signal to her he knew how to handle this situation, though he had no idea, really, what was going on here. Just this: They had lost their children, and he had been the one to find them. Granted, they were much smaller now, and much older. But he'd found them.

"Listen," he said. "Listen, Scott. What say we get to raking up this yard? We can heap up the leaves and burn them down by the curb, like we used to." He paused, took in a deep breath through his nose. "Remember that smell? Burning leaves in autumn. Nothing like it. Remember?"

"Nope," Scott said. He brought the remote down to his lap, switched it to his other hand. "I have no idea what you're talking about."

"Leaves, remember? Me and you leaning on rakes and watching leaves burn."

"How do you lean on a rake?" Scott said.

"I seem to recall trying to accomplish something here, people," Jennifer said then. She was on her hands and one knee now, the other leg going out to the side and back in with the beat of the music.

"You never raked leaves in your life," his wife said to him, and he looked at her. She was looking at him, her eyebrows knotted, face tilted slightly, as though she might not know him. "I was the one out here raking—"

"The hell you were," he said to her. "I used to come out here and rake up—"

"So you started anyway," Jennifer said. She was standing again, doing another dance with her feet. *Feel it in your thighs!* the instructor shouted.

"As would be expected," Scott said. He hadn't yet stopped on a station long enough for a complete sentence to be heard.

"Do you mind?" Jennifer said, and now, finally, she looked up at them both, put a hand up over her eyes to block out the light. She didn't stop dancing, didn't slow down.

"Mind what?" the wife said, and glanced at her husband.

He said, "Mind what?"

"The light," Jennifer said, and turned back to the television. "I can't see the TV for the light out here."

"Not to mention the fact you can't hear a thing for the conversation out here, too," Scott said. He switched hands with the remote again. He did not look up at them.

"But what about your hair?" the wife said.

"What about burning leaves?" the husband said.

"I think," Scott said, "I'd rather watch TV than lean on a rake." He paused, seemed to smile to himself a moment. He said, "Must have been somebody else, some other neighborhood kid you burned leaves with."

"Having a pixie," Jennifer said, "was great. I never had to bother with barrettes and combs and stuff." Now she started doing lunges, her right leg back, the left out in front of her, her body leaning forward as far as she could. *Feel that quadriceps burn!* the peppy woman said. "Stack perm's even better," Jennifer said. "Just pick it out, and I'm done."

"Now," Scott said, "if you'd just put us back where you found us, we could all get on with our lives." With his free hand he made a vague wave back toward the shed.

"Sounds like a plan," Jennifer said, and switched legs, leaned forward now over her right leg. She was looking at the television again.

Slowly the wife stood. Then the husband stood from where he'd knelt next to the cooler.

They looked at each other.

"Well," the wife finally said, "you found them. You're the one who knows where they go."

He looked at her a long moment. He said, "But don't you think we ought to—"

"Top shelf, between the lantern and the paint can," Jennifer said.

"And if you close the handle I can catch the last couple minutes of *Headline News*," Scott said, then, quieter, but just loud enough for everyone to hear, "provided this aerobics crap doesn't drown out the news of the world."

"Just because you sit on your butt all day long doesn't mean the rest of the world has to," Jennifer said. She was working her arms now, pumping them up and down while still dancing. "Just because—"

"Just knock it off, the both of you," the father said.

"Close the lid!" Jennifer and Scott shouted together.

"Fine," the father said. "Fine with me," he said, and quickly knelt, slapped closed the lid. He picked up the cooler without looking at his wife, walked back into the shed, lifted the cooler, and slid it into place between the Coleman lantern and the paint can.

He took a step back, dusted off his hands. He listened for a moment, something small and sharp twisting in his heart while he did so. But he heard nothing, not even the small dark pounding he'd heard when he'd come in here a few minutes before. Suddenly it seemed that the dark inside this shed might swallow him whole, and he quickly turned from the shelves, headed for the light outside.

She stood holding her hands, watching the shed, and here he came, her husband, moving fast from inside that darkened door into the sharp light out here. She saw his face, saw the lines beside his eyes and across his forehead, signs he was aging in just those moments he was heading toward her.

She said, "Well?" though she wasn't sure what she meant by the word, wasn't sure what sort of answer she expected to elicit from him.

"Well what?" he said back to her, the only sensible thing he could think of to say.

He didn't stop when he reached her, only glanced up at her,

saw she was squinting at him for the sun. But in just that glance he believed he saw fear in her eyes, dark and opaque.

Then he was at the window, walked on into the living room. She was right behind him, and as he headed to the kitchen, he heard the window hiss through its track, his wife pulling the window closed.

He went to the sink, looked out the window to the swimming pool, the tarp pulled halfway off. He could see, too, out past the pool, huddled inside the trees back there, the shed.

Now his wife stood beside him, and he saw out the corner of his eye her hands on the edge of the sink, holding on.

They stood side by side. Something had happened here, they both knew. Something huge. And they knew, too, without a word between them, that what had happened was already over, had come and gone.

He said, "What were we fighting about, anyway?"

She said nothing, only shrugged.

Then she said, "Listen, honey." She paused, said, "Listen, Bill, we have to talk." Still she looked out the window, saw more leaves gathering across the surface of the pool, all those withered and empty leaves caught on the water.

He turned to her. He blinked, looked at his wife. He said, "My name's not Bill."

She turned to him, looked at her husband.

He said, "It's Linda, right?"

She blinked. Slowly she shook her head, and he saw her chin start to quiver. "Nope," she said.

They looked at each other a long moment, then turned back

to the window. Now there would be this issue to resolve, they both knew, and the ensuing fight over who was who here.

But for now they were silent.

She touched at her hair, felt the softness of it, mixed in with it a certain coarseness. Old age, she knew, and now she started braiding it as best she could, her eyes never leaving the shed out there.

He watched the shed, too, while more leaves fell, the pool surface nearly covered now. He watched, and thought of the work skimming off all those leaves would be; thought, too, of how huge a bonfire all those leaves would make once he'd gotten them heaped out on the curb.

THE DIFFERENCE
BETWEEN
WOMEN AND MEN

LATER, SHE PILED EVERYTHING UP IN THE CORNER OF THE ROOM. The armoire she'd had to leave in its place, the huge piece of furniture centered against the far wall of the bedroom. But she'd managed to move their bed across the room, inching it one end at a time across the hardwood floor until it was nestled in the corner, her side of the bed and the headboard touching the walls. She picked up the small table she used as a writing desk, set it upside down on the bed, pushed it to the wall, then set the cane-seat chair on the bed, too.

Next came the dresser drawers, each pulled out and set one on top of another next to the table on the bed, four drawers filled with her clothes stacked on the bedspread. Then she pulled the empty dresser itself across the floor, the dresser top littered with barrettes, bracelets, bottles of perfume on her side; on his side a comb, an ashtray, three AA batteries, and a small red rock from somewhere she could not recall. She pushed the dresser up along the footboard until it, too, touched the wall.

Finally there were only the odd items left on the floor: the clock radio from on top of the desk, still plugged in, *9:42* blinking in red; the black three-legged nightstand, more a stool than anything else, and the lamp that sat on it; the assortment of clothes she'd intended to drop off at the dry cleaners someday: two rayon skirts, a silk blouse, three sweaters that'd been ready to go since October. There were some of his things mixed in, too: a blue cardigan, a pair of gray wool slacks, a sweater-vest.

She gathered up the clothes, made her way across the room to the bed, her footsteps on the floor strange and loud now that the room seemed empty, everything in the corner.

Except the armoire, centered there at the far wall, inside it all of his things, and now, suddenly, it seemed fine that she hadn't been able to move it. Nothing in it was hers. Only his.

This was when he came into the room, stopped just inside the threshold. Already she could smell him, felt on the air in the room the cold he'd brought with him from outside.

She smiled at him, let the clothes drop to the bed.

He said, "What are you doing?" and his words, like her foot-steps across the room, were strange and loud to her. He still had his jacket on, still had on the muffler and his gloves. And he smelled of the eight or ten cigarettes she knew he must have smoked out in the car, where she'd left him before coming up here to move furniture.

It came to her, the answer to his question. She'd known for the last half hour, ever since she'd slammed the car door shut in the garage, then slammed behind her the door into the laundry room, that at some point he'd pose the question he had: *What are you doing?* Until that moment she'd had no answer ready, no reason she could see for doing what she'd done. She was simply moving furniture, what seemed to her the only logical thing to do after what he'd told her on the way home.

Or what he'd tried to tell her: the difference between women and men.

She looked at him, and it occurred to her that this man, her husband of twenty-seven years, was a strange and loud man, stranger and louder than any man she'd ever known.

Moving furniture is what I'm doing, she thought to tell him, but the words came out: "You are a strange and loud man."

"What?" he said, and left his mouth open. He took a step closer to her, then stopped. "What did you say?"

"I said," she said, "I'm moving furniture."

She went to the clock radio, unplugged it, carried it to the bed while wrapping the cord around it. She said, "What did you think I said?" She set the clock radio on top of the clothes in the top dresser drawer.

He took another step into the room. "I—" he began, and stopped. From the corner of her eye she could see him working off first one glove, then the other. "I'm—" he began again.

"No need," she said. "Apologies not accepted," and she reached inside the lampshade, twisted off the black knob. The room was dark then, the only light that from the hall, what fell through the open door behind her husband. He was only a silhouette now, big and vague.

She stooped, unplugged the lamp, brought it to the bed. Fifteen cigarettes, she thought then, smelling him in the darkness, that smell growing louder and stranger, his silhouette growing bigger and more vague the longer he was in here with her. He'd smoked a whole pack out there, she thought, and set the lamp on the cane seat of the chair.

"I believe I'd rather we discuss the matter," he said, and she heard the rustle of the muffler as he pulled it from around his neck, heard the first buttons on the jacket unsnap. "As your husband—"

"You are a big and vague, loud and strange man," she heard her own voice give out, words she'd had no idea were leaving her.

The buttons stopped unsnapping, and she saw his silhouette, frozen against the light from the hall.

She picked up the nightstand, carried it to the bed, laid it atop the clothes for the dry cleaners.

He said, "What did you say?"

"I said," she said, "I believe I'd rather move furniture."

But now she was done. In the light from the hall she could see that she'd piled everything up in the corner of the room, that everything she could move had been moved. Except his armoire.

She looked from the armoire to him, put her hands on her hips. What words would come from her now? she wondered.

She said, "Please move the armoire." They were words she'd planned herself, words she'd made on her own.

He turned from her, looked to the armoire. She could see his profile in silhouette now, and he seemed to grow even more vague, even bigger.

He looked at her. He said, "But my back." He paused. "You know my back. My back."

She watched him reach a hand behind him, touch his back.

"Move the armoire," she said, her own words again.

"But—" he said, and he took a step toward the light from the hall, toward the open door behind him.

She walked across the room to the armoire then, her steps

suddenly quiet and sensible, him so big and vague and strange and loud. He'd smoked a carton of cigarettes out there, she knew.

Then she knelt next to one end of the armoire, centered there against the far wall.

She looked back to his silhouette one last time, saw him stopped in the doorway.

Her arms holding tight to the huge piece of furniture, she then lifted the armoire with a miraculous ease, lifted it and lifted it, the armoire no heavier than a blue cardigan, a rayon skirt. All his things, just like that.

The top of the armoire bumped the ceiling, made a quiet and sensible sound in the darkness. She let the piece of furniture down a bit, then brought it up to bump the ceiling again.

She looked at him. He was out in the hall now, and she could see his face in the light out there, his mouth still open. The gloves were on the floor next to him, his muffler hanging loose in one hand, the jacket still half unbuttoned.

"A quiet and sensible sound," she said, and they were still her own words. She bumped the armoire against the ceiling again. "Wouldn't you agree?"

He said nothing.

She said, "Where would you like this?" and started toward him with the armoire containing all his things, then lowered it so as not to scrape the top of the doorway on her way out of the bedroom.

She would sort out the dry cleaning things later, she knew, then clear off his side of the dresser. But right now there was this business of the armoire, and where to put it.

Everything Cut Will Come Back

MY BROTHER PHONED FROM CALIFORNIA. WHEN I HEARD HIS voice, I thought of the wide, clean streets, the homes bright and airy, the yards green. I'd spent the day hanging out the second-story windows of my home, knocking icicles from my gutters. I'd shoveled the porch, driveway, and sidewalk, then spread salt over ice my shovel could not break. In California it was two on Saturday afternoon, and sunny. Here it was five at night, and dark. Snow fell.

My brother: Tim the salesman. The boy who couldn't wait to get out of western Massachusetts, couldn't wait to give up this place to go—for no better reason than that he wanted to go—to California, and find what his life would give him.

He calls me, and we talk, and there's never anything between us that keeps us from our hearts. That sounds cheesy, I know. But it's what's kept us alive as brothers all these years, me here and as sure of why I stayed as he was sure his life was to be lived a continent away. Our parents are dead, killed in the kind of lucky turn of tragedy some people only hope for: Once we two boys'd been married off—Tim to Judy, a girl he met out in California; me to Susan, who I met at UMass—and after we'd found our means, and before any grandkids were born to miss them, they died one summer evening in a car accident driving home from a weekend away at a bed-and-breakfast off the Mohawk Trail. They both had been asleep, the coroner told us, when the car left the roadway.

Now and always, it seemed, here we were: brothers.

We had a bad connection, most everything repeated some- where along the line, so that his voice sounded as if he were speaking through cellophane. I asked him how the weather was. There was the pause at his end as he took it in. "Sunny, sunny," he said. "In the eighties."

He was quiet again, and I pictured him inside his home, sit- ting in his black recliner. He looked out the picture window be- hind the television set at his close-cropped backyard, rosebushes neatly trimmed, sycamore filled with green leaves.

"I called to tell you something," he said. "Lew's wife died. Betty. This morning."

I paused then, too, and took in his words: Lew's wife died. This morning.

Lew, my brother's next-door neighbor. He was tall, about six-two, and thin, his white hair slicked back on the top and sides. His eyes were gray, and he was in his seventies. I thought of his bad teeth, and how I didn't mind them at all because of the easiness of his smile. I knew Lew. I'd met him a few times, every time we went back to visit.

And I thought of Betty, and found it difficult to picture her. She had had a stroke, I remembered, some three years ago.

"Massive brain hemorrhage," he went on. "She'd been in the hospital three weeks. She had it at three in the morning, the hem- orrhage. Police, fire trucks, the works came out for it. Judy and I watched the whole thing from the bedroom. We thought they'd had a fire or something." The word *something* echoed twice on the line, this bad connection.

I was sitting on the bed in the bedroom upstairs and watched, through the window, flakes fall past the light post outside, the snow illuminated for a few seconds, then slipping out of sight. I imagined I could hear flakes landing, a soft static sound, but realized it was static on the line.

"He called her his bride," my brother said, "every time he introduced her to anyone. 'This is my bride of forty years,' he'd say."

He was quiet. I heard my wife moving around downstairs, doing something. I heard my two children laugh somewhere in the house.

"Are you okay?" I said.

"Oh yeah," he said, too quickly. "Oh yeah."

I said, "Go on."

"I was mowing the yard," he said. He hadn't hesitated a moment. "This morning, about seven, when Lew pulls up. He sat there in the car a minute after the motor's off, and I knew she was gone. I could just tell. He didn't even have to get out of the car before I could tell. I cut the mower right then, turned it off. We used to mow our lawns together, I was thinking right then. We used to get up every Saturday morning and do our lawns, match each other stroke for stroke up and back. We both had Bermuda in the front, and we'd have our own contests to see who could cut his lawn closest without losing the green. I was thinking about that."

And I was thinking about how my brother tried to make it as

a gardener once, how he had mowed lawns, landscaped, planted sod, torn out sod, rototilled for the first two years of his marriage, until Judy took him into the kitchen of their apartment one evening, laid the checkbook out in front of him, and showed him there was no money. He'd had a pickup and an old trailer back then, and a front-throw reel mower for close-cut grasses, a rear-bag mulching mower for thicker. A gas edger, a Weed Eater, a lawn roller, a drop spreader: as many different garden tools as he could afford.

"Azaleas," he said then, the word out of the silence and static and snow falling here and sunshine where he was. "Azaleas everywhere. In the flower beds in the front yard, along the sidewalk, next to the mailbox. Flower boxes under the front window. He had them in the backyard, too, against the back fence. Bordering the patio. In boxes back there, too. Azaleas."

I tried to picture azaleas, but could not. And it seemed in that moment, my brother giving to me his heart from three thousand miles away, a betrayal. Azaleas. What did azaleas look like?

"All colors," he said, "violet, white, pink, red. Azaleas everywhere. Because Betty loved them. When those things blossomed, the whole yard went crazy. So much color, those bushes like pink and white fires. Blazing violet."

I heard in his voice a blaze of sorts, a blaze of earth, of greenery, of growth, pruning, growth again. "When do they bloom?" I asked. "Are they in bloom now?"

"No, no," he said. He sighed. "Not now. It's winter."

·   ·   ·

Summers when we were kids, Tim spent in the garden, the strangest kid any of my friends'd ever seen. While we were on our bikes off to the woods to build forts or to the quarry to swim, Tim was there out back of our house, tilling the ground, ending up with more zucchini than we could ever eat, and ears of corn he sold out on the road in front of our house, and a few pumpkins too, and watermelons that never really got any bigger than a football, and sometimes peppers, sometimes green beans. The weirdest kid on our road, I always thought, and pedaled away hard.

So it was no surprise at all that he'd wanted to move to California, where things grew year round, where daylight lasted years, where all you had to do was put a stick in the ground and it'd bloom. It was what made him happy, a kind of happiness that gave our parents a certain sad joy I'd seen as he drove off down the same road he'd set up his corn stands on the last two weeks of July every year. The same one I pedaled furiously away on.

Me? By then I knew this was where I wanted to stay. I had my friends here, had started working at the paper as a stringer. And I'd met a girl named Susan.

And after Tim had sold his equipment, he found a job as a merchandiser for a soda pop company, building displays and filling bins on the soda pop aisle, until he moved to relief salesman, covering for those regulars gone on vacation. From there he received his own route, and we knew he wouldn't be back. He'd met Judy by then, and married her, his life in motion full and hard all the way out there in California.

He was a good salesman, knowing something about planning, about the right time to ask for the right sales, about the cycles of things. I thought it silly when once he explained these things to me, telling me that there were indeed delicate theories and ideas surrounding his profession. Sales is an art, he told me, a pure art, when it's done correctly, like bonsai trees, rock gardens, landscaped yards: There were the right moves, the right approaches, just as there were the wrong ones. Cut one branch too close, the tree withers. Lie about case cost to a manager once, lose sales later. He knew about planting, about waiting, about trimming and pruning back. He knew when to bring in only a few cases, and when to truck them in by the ton.

A few years later, he was able to afford a home of his own, with a yard. And in that yard he brought to play these theories in the way he'd always wanted: the close-cropped grass, the pruned rosebushes, the shaped bushes and trees.

"I thought about what it was he had growing in his yard," my brother went on. "The Bermuda there in the front, Saint Augustine he had growing in the back, that stuff with the wider blades, the thick stuff you need to cut just as close as the Bermuda."

I nodded, and he started in again, as though he'd seen me.

"And the trees he had over there were all things you could eat, I was thinking. In the front yard he had an olive tree, around to the side yard a plum tree. In the back he had dwarf lemon and orange trees in those oak half barrels. He had an avocado tree, and a peach tree back there. And against the other side of the house he had a grape arbor. Just a trellis, but Lew liked to call it his arbor."

Then he gave a laugh, small and quiet, the sound across the line like some foreign language. "The first time I tried any of those grapes," he said, and I could hear him smiling, "Lew brought over a bunch the size and color of peas and told me I had to taste them, that he'd already had some. He pulled off three or four and popped them into his mouth. I put a dozen or so in my mouth. I bit down. They were hard as acorns, and sour. I spit mine out. Lew laughed and swallowed his. 'Terrible,' he said, and he was laughing. 'Rotten.'

"We even tried the olives once. They were tough and greasy, but they tasted like olives. And the avocados never got very big. But there'd been the oranges and plums and lemons and peaches, bags of them he brought over whenever any of them came ripe. Most of the time I'd ended up dumping half the fruit in the garbage. But how could I turn him down? How was I supposed to do that?"

"Who's that?" my wife called from downstairs.

I put my hand over the receiver, brought it down to my lap. "Tim!" I yelled.

"Oh," she said. "Well, say hi."

I put the phone back to my ear. Outside, snow still fell. "Susan says hi."

"Oh," he said. "Say hi back." He took a deep breath, as if he were thinking not about my wife but about his question, as though he were wondering how he could have turned down such a gift as all that fruit.

"You couldn't turn it down," I said. "The fruit. It would have rotted in his yard if you hadn't taken it. You did him a favor."

"True," he said. "He told me it was Betty wanted the trees.

She wanted trees that would grow things you could eat. That's why he'd planted everything."

We sat there for a few moments, quiet. Then my brother started again.

"He used to bring her out in the sun while we worked on our yards Saturdays. He'd set up a lawn chair in the middle of the driveway, then walk her out and set her down in the sun, and we'd have at it. She sat there without moving, you know, because of the stroke and everything, and she watched us."

I heard his voice crack then, a slight falter. He took in a breath.

"Some nights I'd lie awake and think about what it would be like," he went on, though quieter, slower. "What it would be like to have those things to worry about: the yard, the trees, all those azaleas. Sometimes I'd get up and look out the bedroom window at Lew's backyard and just wonder. And I'd start envying him, even though he had a wife who'd had a stroke, who he had to take care of all the time." He paused, took in another breath. "He fed her," he said, his words even smaller and filled, I could hear, with a quiet kind of awe. "He washed her hair. He took her to the bathroom. He taught her to walk again. Every day for seven months he made her get out of bed and take a step, one more each day. Seven months it took her to walk all the way to the kitchen."

Then he was quiet. A car passed by outside, almost silent on the new snow.

"But is that so bad?" he said. "Is that a sad thing to have to do? Nights when I was looking at those fruit trees down there it seemed to me he was just carrying out what he wanted to do in the first place, back when he'd married her. He was finishing what he'd said he would forty years ago. He was finishing his love for her."

I said, "You did the right thing. Taking that fruit." I paused, and heard how empty the words were, yet even in that emptiness I said it again: "You did the right thing."

He wasn't talking about fruit, I knew. And he knew it too.

"So what I did was this," he said, and I was thankful in that moment for his forgiveness, for the way my hollow words were already gone. "It'd been three weeks since Lew had touched his yard," he said, "not since Betty'd gone to the hospital. He'd spent the last three weeks at the hospital. He'd already gone into the house by this time, and so I pushed my mower out onto the sidewalk and went over to Lew's, and went in on his lawn. It was all I could think to do. I had at it. I mowed his grass as close as I could, then mowed it again. Then I took out the edger and went all the way around the yard. Then I turned the dirt in the flower beds, swept everything off—the sidewalk, the driveway, the porch—then I hosed everything down. I could feel Lew watching me all this time, somewhere in the house, but I didn't care. I was thinking about the lawn, about how it still didn't look right, something still didn't look good about it.

"So then I went around to the side gate and let myself in, wheeled the mower and edger in, and had at the backyard. I gave it the same treatment as the front. I never cut grass any lower in my life, I swear it.

"And all this time Lew's back there in the house, watching

me, I can tell. I felt like he was right there with me, right behind me sometimes, watching me weed the beds, trim the yard, dump grass into barrels. Sometimes I'd look out the corner of my eye to the sliding glass window onto the porch, but I never saw him. I just kept on."

He was quiet again, but now I heard something. At first I thought it was the radiators in the house beginning to steam up, to whistle before they let loose. But I listened closer, and heard my brother crying.

I said, "You know, we love you," meaning, *I love you*. Instead of saying that, I'd put some of the responsibility onto my wife, my children. "We love you," I said again.

He cleared his throat, went on as though I hadn't said a thing. "Things still didn't look good. I thought a good trim and cut and weeding would do the trick, but it didn't. So I went to my garage and got the garden shears. That was it, I knew. Things had to be cut back. Things were shaggy. I started with the oleanders along the left fence. Then I got a pair of pruning shears and cut back the rosebushes against the back fence. They didn't really need it, but I still cut the hell out of them. And each snip, each branch falling back, made me feel better.

"I finished that, and then I started in on everything else in his yard. I cut everything back. I knew he was watching me, but I didn't look to see if I could catch him. I cut back the avocado tree, the peach and plum trees. I cut back branches until it looked like dead winter and some big storm'd torn leaves, branches, everything off. I went back to the grape arbor and cut the hell out of everything back there. Everything I cut will come back,

I was thinking. It'll all come back in a matter of time. And then I went at the azaleas. I got down on my knees and started working them over, trimming and shaping and trimming, and that was when Lew came out."

He took a breath. "I looked up from a flower box, and there he was, his arms crossed, his head lowered. He didn't look at me, only at the bushes. He nodded, and I went on. I didn't say anything.

"He went around the yard then. He went to the arbor and touched the branches, went to the orange tree and put his hand around the trunk. He squatted down and ran his hand across the grass, that grass I'd cut so short. Then he came over and watched me finish shaping the azaleas. Then I led him out into the front yard and started working on the azaleas out there. We never said a word. He just watched me. And then I came home."

I said after a moment, "Good." I said, "You did the right thing." Those same empty words as before, still just as empty.

Still nowhere near what he was talking about.

We were quiet. Static rose on the line, snow fell, the sun shone. I watched the clock on the nightstand, watched the red numbers change three times—*5:21, 5:22, 5:23*—without a sound between us.

And then, as though the words were preordained by the incalculable weight of winter here and sunlight there, he said, "I miss them."

"Me too," I said, without a moment of pause, and we both knew, without anything other than the silence to pass between us and these small words, that we were touching the loss of our parents, the world delivering us by whatever means possible the means by which you will find love.

Even in loss, you will find it.

Here was what he was talking about: love, and grief. Both as pure and true as sunlight and snow.

I said, "I love you," and the echo on the line brought it back to me. *I love you.*

"I love you, too," he said, and I saw my brother, sitting in his recliner, looking out a window on the same world I knew. This one. Ours, made so by the history we shared.

We talked a little longer, about his job, about Judy, and then we got off the phone. I looked outside. The snow had stopped.

I went downstairs to the living room. My wife sat on the sofa, reading a book. My two children were lying on the carpet, a newspaper spread out before them. They were clipping things out of the paper: articles, ads, photos. They looked up at me, smiled, and went back to whatever it was they were doing. Susan turned to me.

"What did he have to say?" she said.

"He wanted to tell me a story," I said. I shrugged. "I can tell it to you later. What are you reading?"

"Nothing," she said. "Trash. You wouldn't want to know." She smiled.

And then I smiled back to her, and I looked at my children, my wife, this house. All moving, living, breathing.

All of them stories.

And because they were living their own stories, and because

I loved them all, and loved my brother, and my parents, and loved this house and the snow outside and my life, I did the only thing I could do: I went to the closet, put on my coat and gloves, and told my wife and children I was going to the market for some milk and eggs. Susan told me we had plenty of milk and eggs. I said, All right, I'm going for bread and juice. But, she started, and I kissed her before she could say anything.

Outside it was almost as light as day for the way streetlights banged up off the snow. I started the car, got out and brushed snow off the windshield and rear window, then went for a drive.

It was all I could think to do.

I drove up into the hills outside of town, back to the empty fields and rows of empty tobacco barns, my car moving quietly across the snow. I passed cornfields and tobacco fields and pasture, the snow violet in the dark. And I thought of how, a few months from now, those fields would be green with rows of corn, and later in the summer big-leafed tobacco plants would come up, and only a few months later, young people from town would harvest it all. The green would be gone, and here would be the snow again.

I turned the headlights off and drove along, the car, it seemed, even quieter now. I tried to picture, as I had a million times before, my parents driving a summer road through the Berkshires, holding hands after a weekend away, their children grown and gone and themselves on their way home one last time.

And I saw them, saw their hands together, and saw, too, love.

The road lay before me, a narrow violet ribbon through the hills, my headlights still off, and I knew that whatever way I went, whichever turn I took, that road would lead me home. I just had to be careful, to stay awake, to let the road be the road, and me the traveler on it, though there was in this realization no lesson from my parents' having lost their lives by leaving the road. Only that mine wasn't over yet, that the road before me was ready to take me where I was loved, and where I loved.

And I drove.

HISTORY

THERE HE WAS: ROGER. MY SECOND SON. MY BABY BOY. IT WAS him. Really.

But it wasn't, of course. Not here at O'Hare. He was home in Charleston, where he works and has his family set up: Marlene, and the two girls, my granddaughters: Susan and Jeannie. I knew that, knew he wasn't here in Chicago. I'd just talked to him a week or so ago, and he hadn't said word one about traveling anywheres, though he does travel a good deal.

But for a second or two I believed it was him, there at the gate across from me sitting here and chewing on a bagel with cream cheese out of a tiny plastic container, like you'll get butter in, and I looked up from the fact sheets on the cookie line I'd just taken on, the point of my trip, really, these cookies and whether or not I could take on another line, sell them to Winn-Dixie or Harris Teeter or Piggly Wiggly once I got back to Orlando, where I live and work as a food broker.

Boyce, my husband, Roger's father, is gone. He died two years ago.

But for that minute or so it was him, Roger, there at the gate and letting the ticket agent have it for whatever reason. Roger, a good three inches taller than his father and with that skinny beard and hairline working back on him, that gray hair at the sides, gray just like his father's. Roger, overweight, slouching like he does because he's as tall as he is, and wearing those same clothes he always does: flannel shirt and tweed jacket and khaki trousers. Uniform of the profession, of course. He's a history teacher, and gives papers at minuscule conferences all over the country on Charlemagne and his cohorts, hence why he travels, and hence, too, why I thought for that minute or so it really was him. Roger, gone to give another paper on his hero, Charlemagne.

Then he turned his back to me, this piece of bagel in my mouth now like a wad of warm wax, my baby boy at the gate across from me, and I saw the bald spot at the back of his head, and I figured only then it wasn't my son but somebody else. Though Roger's hairline is retreating on him, he doesn't have a bald spot, I know that much.

So it wasn't him.

He turned back to the agent, a wiry kid with perfect blond hair who was staring at the monitor just below the countertop, and started in on him again. He had a ticket in his hand, this man I'd thought was my second son, and shook it just a little, then put a hand to his hip, tilted his head, let keep coming the words he wanted to give out to the blond kid. His eyebrows were jammed together in the middle, I could see, his mouth inside that beard and mustache working away, that ticket quivering not twelve inches from the kid, who only stared at the monitor, his hands working, I guess, at the keyboard down there.

And darned if this man didn't even argue like Roger does, the way he tilts his head, hand on his hip like he owns the world, and you, measly you, and the problem you've given him, are the source of all the strife on planet Earth. That way.

Just like his father. And I saw in that moment that, of course, Boyce was the one used to hold his hand on his hip, and I knew then too what I'd known since Roger was a child and held his hand on his hip in just that way, tilted his head when he'd had enough of me and wanted that third cookie or to ride his bike one more time around the block: It was his father I was watching, or might as well have been. Boyce. Him, in my son.

I live outside Orlando in a huge apartment complex not a mile from the airport. There's a pool there, a Jacuzzi hot tub, a sand volleyball court, barbecue pits, et cetera. The apartment itself is a small thing, a single bedroom and a bathroom, a kitchen and living room, all of it painted white once a year by the real estate company that owns the entire operation. There's a garage, too, one of a hundred in a long row set apart from the apartments themselves, and I sometimes forget which one is mine, just start pressing the garage door opener on my visor once I get close to where I think it ought to be, and look for the one that lifts up. That one's mine, and I pull in, maybe two feet on either side of the car once I'm in, then pop the door closed on the visor, go out the back door of the garage to a little garden area planted with ivy, and to the front door of the apartment.

It's smaller, of course, than the house, which I sold off right after Boyce died, because it was what seemed the right thing to do: streamline. The kids—Roger; his older brother, Dean; and Linda, the firstborn—had all moved out years before, though after Linda got divorced she moved back home with Kevin and Sasha in tow, her two boys, my grandsons, her job at the accounting firm in Orlando nowheres near enough to let her live on her own. That lasted three years, until she met up with Jack, married him, and moved out on us.

Then, of course, Boyce died, and here was this empty house we'd bought for $28,000 in 1974, and which I could sell for $150,000—$112,000, once the real-estate agent and the balance on the mortgage was paid off—and no more worrying over cleaning a house growing bigger and more empty each year, Boyce and I living in only the same three rooms: kitchen, living room, bedroom. After he died there was then the yard and the pool for me to worry over. So it seemed the right thing to do. After I'd paid Uncle Sam off I just split the money four ways, a quarter to each of us.

Then I moved to the apartment, a good half hour closer to the office. And there's that pool I don't have to pay some kid to clean or do it myself.

Streamlining.

But the kids—see, the kids thought what I'm sure everybody thought and still thinks today, two years later, that all of this streamlining was how I wasn't dealing with the center of things: Boyce, his passing on. But they're wrong, and I can prove it.

Because there's these moments, like this one right here at O'Hare, when all of it sweeps back over me, and I'll see some small thing like a traveler tired as I am of traveling wherever it is he's traveled, and I'll see he looks like my son, believe it for a minute or two, then let track back into me that truth of how Boyce used to stand and let me have it, give to me whatever words he'd planned to give.

And here he'll be.

SOMEBODY ELSE

FINALLY, BECAUSE HE WANTED WHAT HAD HAPPENED BETWEEN them finished, he said, "I love you."

"Now you tell me," she said. She stood at the window, holding herself.

He was silent a moment, then said, "Well, yes. Now."

The room was dark save for the pale silver mist cast by the moon. Neither had thought to turn on any of the lights in her apartment.

"It only occurs to you now to tell me you love me." She stood in profile to him, holding herself, her eyes, as best he could tell, looking out the window. It was a second-story apartment, and he could see out the window the small parking lot behind the complex.

She still hadn't put any clothes on, and he saw how the light from the moon shone on her, illuminated her face and breasts and abdomen and arms. The rest of her was lost to the darkness of the room, this woman an apparition, floating in the dark and light of a bedroom.

But he could see enough. He saw in the way she held herself the damage he had already done, saw in the slope of her shoulders the weight he'd placed there. And he saw in this damage and weight his way out.

"It occurred to me to say that before," he said. He'd gotten his underwear on and his shirt, though he still hadn't buttoned it. "But I'm saying it now. I love you."

He stood from where he sat at the foot of the bed, started in on the buttons there in the dark, and as he stood he caught sight of himself in the dresser mirror against the wall across from him.

He turned quickly to look behind him, startled at the glimpse of a dark and ill-defined man in the darkness of the room. For an instant he believed there was a third person here, someone lurking and listening to all that had taken place this evening; but when he saw nothing behind him, he knew in the next instant that in fact it had only been his reflection. He felt his face flush, felt his neck go hot with the knowledge he'd been fooled so easily.

She turned to him. She said, "What? What's wrong?"

"Nothing," he said. "Nothing."

He let his hands go from the work of buttoning his shirt, went to her there at the window. She was facing him, her back to the window, so that she was a silhouette to him, a faceless woman who stood holding herself against the dark and the moonlight.

He put his arms around her, held her close. He smelled her hair, closed his eyes.

He said, "I just love you."

Still she held herself, and he felt her turning in his arms, turning so that now he held her from behind, his arms holding her arms holding herself, the two of them facing the window.

He opened his eyes, saw out the window what she'd been watching: the parking lot, a few cars scattered across it. He saw his car down there, saw hers. He saw the wooden fence at the back of the lot, beyond it the rear of a grocery store, the loading dock there, everything lit with the moon.

"Look," she said, and he saw her hand go to the window, saw her point down and to the right.

Two people were walking away from the apartment building, a man and a woman. They were holding hands, he could see.

The two people walked toward a car at the far end of the lot, an old station wagon parked backwards in the slot, the rear bumper almost touching the fence between the lot and the loading dock.

"I said I love you," he said, and heard in his calculated words the finality of event, the end of things as he wanted them to end.

The couple reached the station wagon, stopped. He saw in the moonlight the woman look up at the man, saw the two of them lean together, saw them kiss.

It was a small kiss, not much more than a peck, he believed, but because it was so brief the kiss seemed to carry with it all the more value, carried with it, he thought, love.

"That's us," she said, and paused. She seemed to take in a breath, seemed to stiffen in his arms. "That's us," she said again, this time in a whisper, "if we were somebody else."

The two people separated then. The man went to the driver's side, the woman to the passenger's. They opened their doors at the same moment, the dome light inside cutting on, a dull yellow light that filled the inside of the car.

They climbed in, and he saw their faces, saw they were smiling. For a moment he thought he recognized them. He thought he knew these people, their faces almost familiar.

Then he knew them, and knew the truth of what she'd spoken a moment before, words uttered by this apparition in his arms, a woman bathed in the silver mist of the moon.

It was, in fact, themselves down there. He knew the woman's smile, knew his own as well, though he could not now recall the feel of one, the twist of muscles beneath skin that might signal some joy, a moment of light.

It was the two of them down there. Him. Her.

Then the car doors closed, and the couple disappeared.

He let go of her. He'd seen enough, and turned back to the room before the car started, before the flare of headlights that would illuminate the world, reveal himself in this room to be only a glimpse in a mirror, an apparition himself.

He worked at the buttons, eyes closed, satisfied now there were no words left.

Then she spoke. "I love you," she said.

He paused, uncertain what she meant by this. He slipped the last button, the one at his throat, into its hole, his fingers suddenly huge and clumsy, ill designed for such detailed work.

He opened his eyes.

Here they were, of course, seated in the station wagon at the stoplight outside the complex parking lot, to his right the grocery store, to his left the complex. The station wagon headlights illuminated the midnight intersection before them.

He turned to her, saw her smiling at him.

He'd thought he would be the one to end this. He'd thought he would have the last word.

But then the light changed to green, and she nodded, still smiling. "It occurred to me to say that before," she said, using his own last words against him, "but I'm saying it now. I love you."

She was the one to finish it, he saw only then. And she was the one, too, to usher him into this next event about to begin, an event over which he had lost control, an event freighted, he knew, with damage and weight.

He took in a breath, held it a moment, let it out. He looked at the green light hanging above them, did his best to will it back to red. But the light stayed green.

Then he looked out his window and over his shoulder, looked behind him to a second-story apartment window.

The window was darkened, but he believed he could see two faces there, both of them vague and ill-defined, gray in the moonlight.

He wanted to recognize them. But they were no one he knew.

"I just love you," she said.

He turned to the woman beside him, saw her eyes.

He tried to speak, but no words came to him, all the words he knew used up, gone.

Then he did the only thing he knew to do, and leaned toward her, moved his face to hers, and gave her lips a small kiss, not much more than a peck, a kiss so brief it seemed to carry with it all the more value, carried with it, he thought, love. A kiss he would have given, he knew, if he were somebody else.

He pulled away from her, felt himself smile: another symptom he was not who he believed he was.

He faced forward, placed his hands on the steering wheel at ten and two o'clock. He looked at her one last time, nodded. Still she smiled at him.

Then gently, carefully, he gave it the gas, eased their station wagon out into the world.

THE TRAIN,
THE LAKE,
THE BRIDGE

WE SAVE THIS STORY FOR ONLY THE DARKEST WINTER NIGHTS, the thickest snows, when we know we cannot dig out for a few days and so are guaranteed one another's company.

Sure, there are plenty of stories we pass back and forth among us. There is the story of Elder Hosmer, dead these one hundred years, and the Hosmer place, about the light that passes from window to window early midsummer mornings. There is the story of the Indian, one of King Philip's men, and how he screams certain evenings from the top of Greenscott Hill, his foot snapped in a saw-toothed bear trap generations ago. And there is the provost (maybe he set the trap the Indian was caught in, we often speculate) and the story of how he walks our creeks and streams autumn nights, his wife's scalp in one hand, his own bloodied hatchet in the other. These are all stories we tell indiscriminately when we are hunting, rifles crooked in our arms as we stand before a blazing campfire at dawn, or walking home nights after town meeting, or after large suppers.

But the story of the train is irrefutable. It happened. We were there: three boys, but boys with enough sense and enough fear to know when not to tamper with the truth. It was the truth that frightened us the most.

As was often our habit during the Great Depression, and as we still do today, our families had gathered together for dinner. It was a night much like this, a night of snow, and by ten-thirty there was no chance of anyone leaving. There had not been much snow that winter, not until that night, but there had been bitter cold, and Shatney Lake had already frozen clear and thick. We were assured of having nothing to do the next day: no work, no school, only the giant task of digging ourselves out, and even then there would be no hurry. The snow was here to stay, and we had no idea when it would let up. We started to bunk down for the night, the men and boys in the front room and kitchen, the women and girls in the bedrooms. We boys settled into our quilts and blankets and waited for the stories our fathers used to tell. They did not fail us. There was nothing more pleasant back then than to be warm and full and to have a frightening story in our heads before falling off to sleep.

And, like every night, we waited for the last train through, a train that made no stop in our small town, but which we counted on every night to rock us gently to sleep, the rhythm of the boxcars like the soft roll of thunder in a summer storm. The train came by, and we closed our eyes, imagining we were on it, riding the rails to destinations unknown, the train rolling along the ridge and slowly curving toward deep, frozen Shatney Lake, then crossing the old trestle, disappearing until the next night, when we would imagine the same things all over again.

But this night, as soon as the rocking of the boxcars disappeared, there came a scream of metal on metal that seemed to last hours, as though Satan had wanted to wake the world on that peaceful night. The scream shuddered up and down the valley until surely every household within four miles had been awakened.

We got up and looked out the windows but could see little, the snow was falling so heavily. Something had happened, we all knew, something terrible. Our fathers decided to go have a look, but our mothers decided otherwise. They would not let the men outside, not in that storm, not in that cold, not in that snow. While they argued the point, we boys climbed out the kitchen window. We were going whether our fathers did or not. We waded through the snow up to the crest of the ridge and to the tracks.

Once there, we looked back to the house and saw a faint yellow glow from one of the windows. All else was white, save for the tracks cleared of snow by the train only a few minutes before. Our fathers would be out here soon, either to find out what had happened or to take us home. We knew.

From the crest we could see nothing around us, but we knew the track from summer days, following it out to Shatney and the bluffs, walking the gravel and rock barefooted, skipping every other creosoted tie. The tracks slowly curved to the lake, and once there on those hot days we would climb down somewhere on the old trestle, drop our fishing lines in, and spend the rest of the day. But these thoughts were far away. We wanted to find out what in God's world had happened.

We reached the lake and stopped dead. There in the white darkness we saw the broken timber of the trestle and the twisted rail torn from the edge of the bluff overlooking Shatney. Had the snow been falling more heavily, had it drifted any more, had we not been looking where we placed each step, the three of us would have stepped off the edge and fallen to the ice forty feet below.

Look, one of us said, pointing off into the snow. He was pointing down. There was something dark there on the lake. We climbed a few feet down onto the ice-covered rocks and stared hard into the swirling, blowing snow. There was something huge and dark and awful down there, something that took on more and more detail as we stared at it, until we realized it was a boxcar. It was a boxcar planted halfway into the ice, hammered into the lake like a spike. It was silent, a dark leviathan in a sea of white snow. We said nothing, only watched the terrible thing standing on end.

And there in the howling wind, the snow stinging our faces, our bodies shivering, the boxcar started to move, slipping slowly down, down, silently into the frozen lake. At first the movement was imperceptible; we imagined it was our eyes or the cold or the play of the snow, but before we could say anything, the boxcar disappeared into the ice, swallowed into the lake as if it were a snake returning to its hole.

Our fathers arrived a few minutes later to find us still there on the rocks staring into the white, none of us having yet spoken a word. We said nothing on the way home, said nothing until we were back inside and near the fire. Our mothers scolded us for having gone, while our fathers looked out the windows, speaking quietly together. We were sent to bed after we drank some coffee, but we could not sleep. The snow continued.

The next morning was bright and clear, and the three of us, having not slept all night, watched the sun rise over the ridge. Our footprints out into the snow had long since disappeared. The snow had drifted so that it took us a good hour just to clear a path from the house to the barn. We fed the horses, which stood in the darkness of the barn, their breath shooting from their mouths like great clouds.

We came out of the barn and saw that our fathers were leaving for the trestle, snowshoes on, day packs on their backs. We came running at them, yelling and crying about wanting to go. It was our right, we reasoned; we had been the first ones there and had seen the last boxcar slip into the ice. In the morning light, the sun banging up off the new snow, the awfulness of that huge black car was wearing off, and the idea of that sunken train in the lake seemed more like an adventure. It was a novelty, something out of the ordinary. We wanted to go down there and look again. They decided to let us go.

Damage to the trestle was greater than we had seen the night before. The bridge had fallen from the bluffs to mid-lake, and the wooden structure looked like some great animal bowing down on its knees. Ice had collected on all the crossbeams and had broken many of the struts in half. We figured that when the engine first moved out onto the trestle, the added weight then broke the already ice-laden crossbeams in two. The engine and the cars following it had fallen in line into the lake.

We stood at the top of the bluff and looked off to where we had seen the boxcar the night before. All that was left to indicate anything had happened at all, that anything had ever been near the lake surface last night, was a sunken area of snow about thirty feet off the edge of the rocks and a little to the right of the bridge. Snow had covered the skim of ice that had already formed in the hole.

Suddenly we heard a whistle blast break clean across the valley, carried across the snow. We turned from the lake to see an engine coming around the last curve before the lake, moving slowly, the prow scraping snow from the tracks as it moved along. The railroad people had arrived.

Only two men had been aboard the wreck, the maintenance supervisor told us. The supervisor was a clean-shaven man and wore blue overalls and shiny black boots. He had on a wool cap and a heavy coat slick with machine oil. Two engineers, he told us, and four empty boxcars coming down from Canada. He told us they had known for a long time that this bridge was a hazard, and that sooner or later the worst was bound to happen, and that they were going to have to close the route anyway, what with the Depression and all. He said it was a terrible shame that it had happened at all, and that it had been these two men in particular. We looked at him for a few moments, then looked at one another.

Then the supervisor broke out several shovels from inside the cab and asked if we didn't mind giving him and his assistant a hand down there on the ice. Railroad policy, he told us, demanded that all accidents be verified, and he had an idea that if we dug away some of the snow from the ice he might be able to verify the engine number, just to make double sure the right train had gone down. The right wives had to be notified of their husbands' demises, the supervisor said.

We took the shovels, as did our fathers, and climbed down the rocks onto the ice. The lake had been frozen a month or so, and we had no fear the ice would not support us. It seemed a foot thick.

We started clearing, keeping a safe distance from the hole where the train had entered. We dug into the snow, clearing an area where the supervisor imagined the engine must be resting, but all we could see through the ice was the cold dark water below. No train. He had us dig in a wider area, enlarging the original borders, and then we stopped digging again. He saw nothing. He asked that we clear a little larger area, nearer the hole, and we did. Our fathers shoveled snow with less and less enthusiasm, but we boys thought it great fun, and with each request of the supervisor dug even more furiously. Still, there was no sign of the train.

After an hour and a half of digging, our fathers quit, saying that the railroad should be damned for sending out good men on a dangerous bridge in the first place. Down on his knees, his hands cupped around his eyes, the supervisor was oblivious and only stared down into the ice.

And then he screamed.

He stood up quickly and slipped on the ice, then tried to stand up again.

"What is it?" we asked. "What is it?"

But before he could answer, if indeed he had ever had any intention of answering, we looked down to where he had been searching and saw a man under the ice, frozen, gray, his arms out to either side in perfect silence.

He wore blue jeans and a red-and-black plaid jacket. He had no face, only a blurred gray area where we expected to see his face.

We all stood there on the ice, none of us moving any closer to what was there under the supervisor. He still screamed and slipped on the ice, calling for our help, for anyone's help. He could not move from his spot above the frozen man.

Then they appeared, first one, then three, then five, all around us, beneath the ice. It took a moment, and then we recognized these men.

They were hoboes, bums catching rides on a southbound train, the same men who hung out of empty cars on summer days and hooted at us fishing from the trestle below them. But these men below us did not move and kept floating to the ice like swimmers seeking air. They appeared from nowhere, and we could not keep them from coming, a dozen, twenty, thirty of them, all bobbing to the surface in different positions, some curled up like stillborn animals, others stretched out straight. They wore overalls and caps and flannel shirts and coats, but none had faces, only blurred, undefined patches above their shoulders. And still they came.

We tried to run on the ice, to get away, but slipped and fell over one another, falling to the ice, our faces meeting the faces of the dead. We screamed, the railroad men screamed, our fathers screamed. We struggled to make it to the snow, to get off the ice and those dead men, those derelicts who had no family except those around them, and who would never receive any burial except that which the lake had given them. We struggled to the snow, almost diving in headfirst when we finally made it off the ice.

And then, just as suddenly, the bodies disappeared, first one, then another, then another, all sinking back to the lake bottom and the train, their home. They seemed to peel away and fell slowly back into the blue.

We did not stay there to figure out what had happened, but moved as quickly and as silently as we could up onto the ice-covered rocks of the bluff, back onto the tracks, and home. The supervisor and his assistant climbed into the cab without a word, the shovels still down on the ice, and backed the engine along the track, first slowly, then faster and faster.

They were gone from the valley by the time we made it home.

The story is finished. There is silence in my living room as everyone here thinks over matters: the train, the lake, the bridge. There are no ghosts to speak of in this story, and it is precisely this fact that frightens us. We have no legends to create around this tale, no stories of old Indians or provosts we can exaggerate. There are no ghosts, except the trestle, still torn and twisted after fifty years, a reminder of our childhood. The train stopped coming through this valley the night of the wreck and has not been back since.

We are no longer rocked off to sleep by the rolling train, but now must put ourselves to sleep, drinking warm milk, reading, or simply staying up all night, assuring ourselves we are alive in this frozen wilderness.

And there is the ghost of the lake, the silence that is taken there. There are no screams at midnight, no candlelight in windows, no blood. We no longer fish there, no longer dare even to set foot in that lake for what we know is buried there. There is only silence.

HALO

HE GAVE THE CASHIER HIS MONEY——A TWENTY AND A FIVE——AND waited for change, the blanket already in the white plastic bag.

He needed the blanket because he knew it would be cold tonight, sleeping in the car. Of that much he was certain: the cold, him in the car, this blanket.

His wife, the woman he'd loved all these years, had kicked him out over what he'd said once they had arrived at the end of the argument: "Whenever I tell you something and you can't remember it, it's because I never told you," he'd said there in the kitchen, certain of the words lined up, certain of the sense they made. Certain, certainly, of the truth they would speak of the way their lives worked. "But whenever you tell me something and I don't remember it," he went on, "it's because I wasn't listening."

He'd said it, there in the kitchen, and he'd nodded hard once at her, put his hands to his hips for the certainty in the world he'd outlined with just those words.

She was quiet a moment, a moment filled, he was certain, with her recognition of his keen and convicting insight into the injustice of her perceptions: She believed her words went unheeded by him, and believed his words had never been spoken. He was certain of all this in just that moment.

And in that moment he was certain he still loved her. He loved her.

But then she spoke. "You understand," she said, and put her own hands to her own hips, and in that movement, a movement that bore extraordinary witness to her own certainty, he'd seen that his own certainty in his own words had been only a vague notion, a moment of smoke. Nothing more.

"Now you understand," she said. "Finally," and she nodded once at him, but gently, carefully, the care she gave the gesture all the more proof of how certain she was.

That was when she turned from him, took the requisite steps to the kitchen door and opened it wide, swept her hand toward the darkness outside like a game-show girl. She said nothing more, so certain she was that he knew what she meant by this move.

And he knew.

He watched the cashier's hands in the drawer, watched the efficiency and certainty with which her fingers extracted the correct number of coins, the single dollar bill, then tore from the register the receipt, handed all of it to him in just one moment. He looked at her hands a moment more, then her face, in him a kind of unbidden awe at the sureness of her hands, of these moves.

Then, the moment over, he took the money, the receipt, lifted the white plastic bag from the counter, and left. She hadn't noticed the moment her hands had been held out to him, or his moment of watching her, and he wondered if in fact there had ever even been this moment between them. Maybe he'd imagined that instant, he thought.

The automatic doors opened, and he stepped out into the

night air, felt the chill and the damp. It would be cold tonight. He was certain of that.

He started off, away from the store and into the lot. His car was here. He was certain of that, too. He would have a place to sleep. And he had this blanket.

He walked, and walked, passed beneath first one parking-lot lamp and then another, each lamp casting thin halos of light down around him while he looked for his car.

He knew it was here somewhere, in this aisle, ten or twelve slots down. On the right. Or maybe it was the next row over. Maybe a few more slots down.

But the lot was nearly empty because of how late it was, and he did not see his car anywhere.

He felt his skin prickling over for the damp out here then, and for the dark, felt how strange and alien this feeling was as he walked, as though his skin were that of someone else, moving on its own in reaction to things out of his control: the temperature of the air, the turn of the earth away from the sun, the ability of air to hold water within it.

He stopped, just inside yet another thin halo of light.

Where was his car?

And did he love his wife still, despite the way words worked in their world?

And then, in the feel of his skin prickling over, and in the growing recognition of his misplacing an item as large and important this night as his car, and in the weight of the blanket in his arm, even in the vague halo within which he stood—a halo, he saw, like words lined up believing in their certainty, only to be found as hollow as his hands on his hips, as empty as a solid single nod—inside all this, he began to wonder:

What made me believe it might be cold at night? And when did I come to believe night would come?

Of what am I certain?

He breathed in, breathed out. He felt himself swallow, though he could not be certain that was indeed what he felt.

Quickly he took the white plastic bag from beneath his arm, held it and what was inside it out in front of him, held it with both hands, his hands trembling now in the smallest way but holding on tight, as if the bag and what was inside it and even his hands, his arms, himself might all disappear this moment.

What do I *know*?

And now he felt even truer, even dearer the earth turning upon its axis, felt deeply and dreadfully himself hanging from this round planet head outward and into space, felt too the wind of all space blow unforgiving and uncaring through him at whatever speed this unheeding planet revolved around the sun, and at whatever speed this unmerciful galaxy blew from its beginning toward its ever-expanding end, felt all of it in just that moment.

Then finally, horribly, he felt fear move inside him, rising, unbidden and awful.

He looked at the bag and his hands and his trembling, looked and looked, and wondered with a deep and incalculable wonder:

What does the word *Blanket* mean?

And what is *Car*?

He looked then to the circle of light in which he stood, saw the asphalt and white lines in this thin light begin to tremble of their own, the world shivering beneath him as sure and certain as the cashier's hands had measured money.

What is *Halo?* he wondered.

And *Moment?*

He looked up to the parking-lot lamp then, felt himself go blind for it, as though scales were being settled into place instead of falling away, while still the earth shivered beneath him, and now the air around him began to swirl, and swirled, and lo! he felt himself lifted, felt himself rising into the pitch and twirl of the air, felt himself lifted and lifted into the vortex of swirling air and shivering earth and incalculable words that surrounded him, until he felt at last each molecule—if there were such a thing, or a word for it—explode into nothing, himself at its center, and nothing. Nothing at all.

What is *Love?* he wondered then. And finally. Finally.

ROSE

—For Mr. Faulkner, with all respect

I

ONCE SHE WAS DEAD, THERE WOULD BE MORE STORIES. SHE knew that, knew how the contemptible commoners of this town thrived on what they could say of her, Miss Emily Grierson. This was a festering town, festered with the grand and luxurious nothingness of small lives that lent them the time, plenty of it, to tell themselves—and the dark of humid evenings filled with the stagnant decayed nothingness of their own lives—tales of her not true, not true, but true because they would tell them to one another, and believe them.

Of course she had killed him. Someday they would know that. But the truth they would never divine. Given all the years of a base and fallen town's life, they could not know the truth: the depth of her love.

She pulled through her hair the engraved sterling brush, black now with tarnish so that his monogram could no longer be read, just as she had each evening since she had given him the comb, this brush, and the other of his toilet articles. Her gift to him that night.

Each night since that night she had brushed her hair before going to bed, hair iron gray now with the passing of years, the same iron gray as her father's when he, too, died so very many years before. Even before she had met the man with whom she had lain, the man she had murdered. Each night, as this night, she brushed her hair by light of the lamp's rose shade as calmly and serenely as she had when, once the man she had lain with was dead, she had risen from the evening summer sheets heavy with the depravity of this life, this town, to find upon the seat of her gown, pure pure white, the small red smudge of red that signaled to her the pain she had felt in their sanctification was indeed real. Then she had simply gone to the dressing table and seated herself upon the chair, its rich burgundy velvet that night thick and rare in its feel, now this night the chair worn smooth to a slick dull red from the years she had sat here each night since.

How many nights? she wondered. Was it last night, when she had lain with him and killed him? A week ago, a fortnight? Or years, decades?

Now?

They would tell stories of her because of the man, dead all these years, in the bed behind her. He would be found out, she knew, with her own passing, when the townspeople would break into her home to find her. They would find his body in the new nightclothes given to him that night upon which she had killed him, him fused into his nightclothes and the bedclothes that had not been changed since that evening a fortnight, decades, moments ago, his flesh no longer flesh but part of the real of this room, as real as the layer of dust on his suit folded neatly over the cane chair at the foot of the bed, on the dresser his tie, his celluloid collar. As real as flesh and bone and love all fused into the sheets, in just the same way lies were fused into the air about this hungry decrepit peasant town filling now—even as she pulled the brush through her hair, as every night—with stories about her.

Let them, she thought. Let them all, in the ugly alchemy of the cracker mind, spawn their bastard lies of her. She knew the truth, knew enough truth to fill the grave, enough to land her in the great bald cold hereafter by dint and force of the truth of love and love and love, love past what any of them could imagine. Then, when each of them met the nothing end of their nothing lives, she would be there on the other side of the muddy disconsolate river of death, and they would see her upon the opposite shore, see she'd crossed pristine and glistening and dressed in pure pure white to the cold bald great hereafter. Then each one of the townspeople, the cretins, who lived upon lies they would tell about her, Miss Emily Grierson, lies savored as a dog savors a bone gnawed to nothing—these crackers would then cry to her for salvation as they themselves tried to cross the disconsolate river, only to find themselves quickly, surely drawn with the ugly weight of their lies of her to the slick silted bottom of the river, their impotent cries to her for salvation and her requisite silence in answer the last reckoning to the truth they would have before their lungs filled with muddy water of the difference between themselves and her that had stood between them their entire living lives: she was of legitimate blood; they were of empty.

II

They were dogs, she knew, every townsman save perhaps the Negro, her boy all these years, the boy now an old man who came and had come and would come with the market basket every few evenings, who swept the kitchen, and the pantry, the hall and parlor, as well as the room in which she now slept.

She did not sleep in this room, this room only a place she visited each night, first to lie down beside the dead man for a moment as best to recapture in the fleshless smile he held and fleshless arms drawn to his throat as if in embrace the beginning of love she'd encountered that night, and next to brush her hair at the dressing table as she had the night love had in fact begun.

She did not sleep in this room, but in a room far more significant than any of these crackers would ever know, could ever know. She slept in the room off the hall downstairs, the room in which, she had been told by her father, her mother had died in childbirth. She herself had been all of her years the only proof positive her mother had ever lived, no pictures, no portraits, not even a moment of clothing or smell or a single strand of perhaps iron-gray hair of her mother's own any evidence her mother had ever existed, save for the words given to her by her father: *Your mother passed in childbirth, giving me you,* he had said to her only once, the day of her fifth birthday, when only then it had occurred to her to ask. He spoke of it not again, ever. Not even her name.

She'd had the Negro move her father's articles from his bedroom the day after she had killed the man and into the downstairs room, the birthing room and passing room, the furniture as big and ungainly as the new secret she held inside her bedroom, the Negro, young then, wrestling mattress and headboard and footboard and night table and dresser along the dark wood walls of the upstairs hall and down the staircase and into the room.

And she had the Negro as well keep her larder full, her pantry filled so that she might eat, and eat, both to hide and to nourish, his trips in with the market basket those days daily pilgrimages, so that even he would not know.

The Negro, she had seen in his eyes when he'd deduced the truth of what had occurred that singular night that would and had and did become every night of her life, was without duty to any but her and her father. A boy born to know his own caste, she knew, born like herself into the life before the War that ended the old life and its way of settling with only the bloodshed of birth who you were on the face of the earth. The Negro was a boy she could—and this was the horrible miracle, after an entire life lived here in this town rent not with the emancipation of the Negro but a town rent, irreparably torn asunder, by the emancipation of the Cracker to become the rulers of this hamlet, the aldermen and mayors and exactors of tax of a generation that did not know its place, that had forgotten the precious gift of a time when order had reigned as it ought to reign, in observance of lineage and standing—the horrible miracle was that now and all these many years it had been only the Negro, unblinking servile Tobe, she could trust.

He had seen things, she knew, and had been trustworthy, had been a good Negro who knew not to let eyes meet and who knew not to question purchases made at the druggist's and who knew not to question as well the smell that had blossomed days after a night that would be the night of all nights in her life.

All nights, save for one. A night even the Negro did not know of, a night beyond reckoning of any sort.

Let the town tell its stories. She had stories of her own.

III

Of the night four weeks and five days after the purchase of the arsenic from the druggist, writ across the package beneath the skull and crossbones the words *For rats* in the druggist's own hand. By then the smell from her bedroom was blossoming horrid and full and genuine, Miss Emily seated on the cracked leather of the parlor's furniture mornings and evenings and afternoons while she ate, and while she stared at the crayon portrait of her father upon its tarnished gilt easel before the fireplace, her father with his iron-gray hair, his mouth closed tight, eyes bright with bearing.

The eyes of a vigorous man. The eyes of a man of will and power.

The eyes of a man who had driven away any suitor who might have delivered her from his eyes, and hence the eyes of a man who kept from her the love she so desired. Until the man in the bedroom upstairs had arrived upon her front porch a year after her father's death.

While the smell blossomed from the room upstairs—could it have been this afternoon? A lifetime ago?—she spent those days in the parlor bearing the stench in the same way she had borne the temper of her father, who had threatened the horsewhip to men who, of a Sunday evening, had made their intentions evident with their appearance at the door of this house, this same squarish house with its balconies and cupolas and spires, still elegant despite the loss of its white paint in blisters popped and peeling back as the man's flesh blistered and popped, left to rot. But the street that had once been the most select of the entire town had grown indigent with itself for all the bearing these new low-slung spireless sheds could hold, sheds that had crept up on her own poised home like the men who had crept up that midnight four weeks and five days after the purchase of the arsenic from the druggist.

She'd spied the men from her window in this room, where she repaired once the day had been spent before her father's portrait, the lamp no longer lit for the dark in which she wanted to sit with her love growing, the man only newly dead then, the smell inside this room a rank blossom too huge and significant and powerless to keep her from staying here in this dark.

Four weeks and five days after the arsenic purchase, the town believing, she knew, the poison was meant for her, her own suicide a kind of expected gift these dullards wanted as a means to give themselves the self-assured nod, to say among themselves, *We knew it. We knew she was crazy after having been jilted by the man.*

But neither had she been jilted, nor was she crazy. She knew, of course, he'd meant to jilt her, but she'd allowed instead the arsenic for him, spooned that afternoon into the bottom of the lead crystal glass in which she poured out bourbon for him once their consecration had been made that night. She hadn't even risen from their bed, only leaned to the small table beside her,

where she had put the glass and decanter in which her father had
kept the bourbon all these years, then watched the man smile at
her in the kind of smile that betrayed a man's lust sated and his
escape begun.

Then his smile twisted into itself, the arsenic quick and swift
and blind in its affections, and she had reached to him, taken the
glass from him before he might drop it and spoil these sheets,
desecrate them with alcohol when they had been so blessed with
the beginning of love only moments before, the two still beneath these sheets as all who have loved with a love as deep as
she had begun to know ought still to be. Then his eyes cinched
shut with the force and grandeur of a poison meting out its purpose, whether for rats or for lovers, and his hands went to his
throat, his mouth an O of lovely pain, beautiful and thrilling
and exquisite pain, his mouth the same mouth only minutes before she had met with her own lips.

She had watched him die, then brushed her hair.

She watched the men down in her yard that night four weeks
and five days after the purchase, watched men look furtively to
left and right, each slung over his shoulder a sack as if of seed,
each man reaching into the bag like a sower and throwing hand-
fuls to the ground beside her house, at the foundation.

Lime. It was lime they were spreading in the ridiculous belief, she imagined, that somewhere on the premises a rat or dog
or some such had died, herself too much the crazy woman to
know or care to dispose of the dead animal and its offenses.

Here was a story she could tell of them: They were fools, all
of them. The smell had come from here, where she sat watching

them work as though they might not be detected. She had seen them here, where love had begun, while they tried as best they could and stupidly to break down love's fiber and being with a handful of lime thrown along the foundation of this house. As if that might kill love.

She relit the rose-shaded lamp then, and seated herself before the window to signal those who would look up at her that she knew who they were, knew why they were here, knew their place. She knew.

One of the elect down there, his hand inside his bag of lime for another handful of lies to spread, turned slowly to her at this window, in this rose-hued light, and then another man came to the first and just as slowly looked up at her in this light as well. The men then moved away from the house, disappeared into the shadows of the locusts that lined the street, the town's elect vanquished as simply and easily as making her presence known, the smell that had drawn them here in the belief they might end it, that sad gift from the man no longer a man but a vessel, a vessel only for love, still just as horrid and full and powerless as it would ever be.

She had sent the signal: I know who you are, and you know who I am.

And you cannot kill the love I know.

IV

She could tell the story of her courtship, so very misunderstood by all, a courtship begun with the negation of all possibility of courtship and hence love, driven away by dint and force of fatherhood.

So that when the contract for the paving of the town's sidewalks was let a year after the death of her father, and the Yankee foreman had knocked on her door of an afternoon to ask smiling after a glass of lemonade, she knew she'd found the sound and shroudless agency of the love she sought. Though he wore a waistcoat and collar and tie, cuffed starched sleeves and herringbone trousers, a straw boater atop his head—every indication of his affluence and enterprise—still his face and hands were tanned from the overseeing of the Negroes hard at work with pick and shovel on the street beyond the shadow of the locusts, the color of his skin betraying the quality of sundrenched toil his job entailed; the solid line of his shoulders and the way that line traced its own vigor gave her to believe he might be enough to hold on to in order to find what she needed; and the color of his eyes, a green so very near and yet so very distant from the green of her father's—gilt green, mordant green—gave her no choice but to see her father, with his horsewhip and temper, there in this Yankee's eyes.

It was then the man winked at her, in that most impudent and improvident blink of an eye something passing from him into her, a cutting shard of possibility, a dagger of prospect, the notion already taking shape in her mind of the agency of love he was to become.

A Yankee. A glorified day laborer. A man so shameless, so arrant as to seek refreshment from a single woman of her bearing—and to wink. Her father would have already made good on his threats with the horsewhip at so vulgar a gesture.

And her father was dead.

There followed the evening visits after his hours in the sun, his arrival at her front door for all this base and common town to see, fodder for more and more stories that would give these dullards life with the telling of them. Sunday afternoons the two rode drenched in the same broad daylight that had perverted his skin to the brown it had become, rode in his yellow-wheeled buggy led by twin bays through the streets of town, her chin high, eyes lighting on no one as they circled the streets, the man's black cigar burning in the glorious and putrid way her own father's had evenings at the dining room table, her food when a child the drenched black and acrid taste of the air as she ate it, a little girl growing and growing toward a resolve to find love that would discover its reward in the man she rode beside, a man with skin too tanned and eyes too near her father's green, that resolve to find love eclipsing the impropriety of their affair, and the impropriety of the man himself.

There followed too his proposal, in secret yet there in the parlor in full view of the portrait of her father on its gilt-easel tarnishing even then, a proposal not for marriage but for fornication, though he'd used the word love upon her, his hands touching her in what she knew was a feigned passion places she had allowed only her own hands to touch.

He did not know what love was; she'd known then and knew it now and knew it all along, his impassioned passionless touch proof enough of his ordination as the one by whom she would find love. He touched her, and though she'd allowed herself small protests at his touching there, and there, and there, she'd found in herself no rising passion at all. Only that resolve: to find love.

Then, as she had known they would, like flitting moths drawn to a flame that would in a moment's touch burn them to ash and air, the town revealed its own ill-bred blood in the impropriety of its admonishment, the town's elect, she had no doubts, sending the Baptist preacher to her door.

The preacher—a dull man, a simple man—let himself in past the Negro one afternoon near a year after she and the Yankee had first been seen together, dispatched no doubt to warn her of indiscretions known to all. She found him seated in the dull afternoon light of the parlor, saw him stand dully as she entered, saw him hold his black hat in both dull hands, his dull eyes daring to meet her own and hold hers, as though the cloth of his vocation were enough to have earned the right to let eyes meet.

She'd held her head high, listened what seemed a lifetime to empty nothings spewed from his mouth like the stagnant decay of evenings in which stories were to be told of her and had been told. She stared at him, head held high, until finally the dull man looked down, his eyes broken by her own.

That was when she turned to the door, drew it open, and made threat to him, on her lips a newfound power, a prayer as old and dangerous and full of horrible promise as the oaths she had heard her father make all her years of possible courtship, oath drawn from the Word and in full ordination of the Christ who oversaw them all—*And when he had made a scourge of small cords, he drove them all out of the temple,* she heard herself say, *and the sheep, and the oxen; and poured out the changers' money, and overthrew the tables*—and felt the instantaneous black joy of such words and knowledge and being, a joy she knew her father himself must have known with each driving of a suitor from their door of a Sunday evening.

The preacher, dull eyes open wide, bovine in his look of genuine low birth for its surprise and awe and terror all at once, was at once gone, stumbling down the stairs off the front porch of the house that was now hers, and not her father's. Yet still the town would not recognize its place: Next came her cousins from Arkansas, dispatched, she would learn, by the wife of the preacher to spend with her days and nights filled with these harpies' presence speaking to her of Grierson lineage and birth and bearing, when only she knew how close she was to finding love, to knowing it, to letting it grow into itself as she had dreamed it might from the moment the idea of love had been given her, and given only once, words ever in her ear and heart and mind, words drenched with the black acrid air of his cigars, drenched in the threat of the horsewhip, drenched in the eyes of power and vigor staring down to her from his portrait across the vast abyss of empty days between her father's death and the appearance of the Yankee: *Your mother passed in childbirth,* came her father's words across the broad expanse of all her days until then, *giving me you.*

The cousins had only left once she'd agreed to end the indiscretion of seeing the Yankee.

She could tell the dullards of this town the story of the courtship that had landed her where she had wanted to be, in the arms of a man as near to her father and as distant as the farthest star. But they would not understand, neither the courtship nor the truth behind fact.

They could not understand the depth of her love.

A courtship none of them would understand, ending as ar-ranged with the appearance of the Yankee at her kitchen door three days after the cousins had left, the Negro admitting the Yankee and then disappearing, leaving the man to find her in the parlor, where she awaited, dressed in an evening gown of pure pure white.

Thus began the night that was to be all the nights of her life. All nights, save for one.

V

She finished now as she did each night with the brush, and turned it over in her hand, scrutinized with her ancient eyes the sterling silver back for the monogram, the tarnish there a kind of black map to the depth of love she had wanted to begin through him, and had begun.

There was the Yankee's monogram, thin lines curled upon themselves like her own ancient fingers curled upon them-selves: *HB*.

Homer Barron, his name had been, Homer Barron, she re-called, and smiled at a name lost each day to the memory of her own life's passing only to be found each night in these same and serpentine black lines in black silver and in the fusion of flesh and bedclothes and nightclothes in the bed behind her, this skeleton and its fleshless grin drawn tight in a new and perfect fleshless smile the same each night, every night.

She stood from the chair, placed his brush upon the dresser, and turned, smiled down in answer to the man, this Yankee, whose name even as she turned was already leaving her, as vague as the outline of her head on the pillow beside his own, so ravaged and peaceful with his accomplished decay.

Once she was dead, she knew, there would be stories, even more, and they would make of the outline, and perhaps the iron-gray strands of her hair she knew must lie there upon the pillow something larger than it was. Let them, she thought. Let their belief of this man and his wiles and her love scorned be the lie they would tell to each other once she was gone. Let them believe she was crazy.

Because there was another story. There was the truth.

She dimmed the rose-shaded lamp as she did each night, and pulled the bedroom door closed behind her, locked it as she did each night with the key she kept on the white ribbon round her neck, then placed a hand to the dark wood of the hall, the feel of the cold walls as close to the feel of a tomb as she might imagine, and then she was at the stairs, descending them one at a time for the age upon her, and for the love she had borne with such regal ease all these years.

The entire world was of empty blood, she knew; only she of legitimate.

Then she was downstairs, and in the hall, all by no more light than a midnight might allow, and now she was at the door to her room, the one in which she slept. The one in which her mother had birthed her and had passed.

Her own room now.

She turned the knob, admitted herself to the room, and saw

in the darkness the white of her bed, the black of the dresser, and the round shape above it that was her lamp, this one rose as well but glass, and she struck a match from the holder beside the lamp, lit it, let the room grow with this rose hue, this warm and reckoning light, then knelt to the bed that had been her father's, the bed in which her mother had birthed her, and in which her mother had died.

A bed of love, she believed, not because of what her father and mother had made here, but because of what her mother had given here, the perfect love she herself had joined her mother in knowing now all these years, the perfect gift she had received upon execution of the covenant she had made with herself, a covenant to find love.

Kneeling, she reached as she did each night beneath the bed, reached and reached, reached as if the loosed board beneath the bed might have of its own accord mended itself, might have made itself whole in a kind of horrible miracle she could not predict but believed might have happened each night she reached for it and could not find it, and then she felt the board's edge, the gap between it and the next, and with one curled finger levered the single board up, all this without seeing it for the rote pilgrimage the search had become all these years. She lifted the board, reached beneath it to touch the corner of the cardboard box, then inched her finger along its side to find the ribbon with which the box had been tied a night so very long ago, a night just last night, a night now upon her.

Her fingers took hold the ribbon and box, slipped it up between the boards, and she pulled it to her until here it was, the square dress box at her knees as mottled and decayed with age as her own hands, the white ribbon the color of parchment, passion finally upon her and rising as new and as ancient as the gift inside she had given herself: love. Here was the only passion worth finding, the only passion worth touching. No other passion existed, save for that rising in her as it rose every night since she had placed the gift here, in the mottled and decayed and beribboned dress box she held.

Slowly, carefully she stood, the box in her hands as though it were the crown of life it was, and laid it on the bed, this bed she and her mother shared in their purpose and design as procreators of the line of legitimate blood. Carefully, gently, she set the dress box on the bed as she set it each night, as every night, even as on the night she herself, Miss Emily Grierson, had borne the child, a night spent alone in this bed and pushing, her body fat with the food she had eaten both to nourish this love and to hide its proof from the Negro, herself the one to remove the bloodied bedclothes and burn them in the cellar furnace, the smoke they might produce evidence further to an ignorant town, a fallen world, that she was crazy for burning the furnace that spring morning, as they would tell one another and believe for the telling of it, her fingernails that self-same night she'd burned the bedclothes digging so deeply into the headboard above her they bled with blood the same red as on the seat of her gown the evening she had made this child with the nameless Yankee— who might well have been her father for the mordant, gilt green of his eyes—her silent and extravagant screams at the relentless pressure below only extravagant in the expanse of her mind as she swallowed them down to nothing in blood-red resolve to find what love is, screams made silent by bearing and heritage and a father with eyes so pitiless and cold she did not know or want to know what the sound of her own voice in rage and blood-filled resolve might sound like.

It was resolve that mattered, the resolve to find love. Not the luxury and pity of a self-indulgent scream.

Gently, slowly, she untied the ribbon as she did each night; slowly, carefully, she lifted free the lid.

There it had been, would be, and was now: the child she had made, nestled inside the gown that had borne the red smudge of red, that red the firstfruits of the child's birth, her beginning of love, though the gown had become the night she had borne the child brilliant with blood, drenched in it, only to become this night as every night she could recall the powerless and caustic brown of old blood.

A baby, withered into the essence of gristle and bone, brown too with blood, its ribs and arms and legs fused into the gown, collapsed into themselves to become the real of the room itself, its skull with its fleshless grin, empty eyes, teeth not yet teeth waiting to form, all here for her to take in and take up as she had each night, and as she would.

Her child. Love. Love so precious she could not, would not allow its presence felt in so fallen a world as the one she now inhabited, a world rent with emancipation into chaos, a world loosed of its reign of history and order and lineage left to wander dully into the void of all time and eternity.

Here was the depth of love the contemptible commoners of

this town could not know: the burden of a family's history in a vulgar world that would shrug history aside, history settled as it was that night and this and those to come always and only with the bloodshed of birth.

She lifted the baby in its once-white nest as she did each night, weightless always in her arms as though history were not the crushing weight it always was, held it close this last moment before she would return the baby to its place hidden from the indigence of this town, her baby's dignity—the whole of her class's history—retained with the secret of its presence kept.

Rose, she whispered now, the name she had given the child the moment after its advent and the moment before its death, that single stranded moment between both when, mouth open in its only inhale and set to scream, the baby ready to hear herself for the first time upon the face of this world, Miss Emily Grierson strangled her, set her free for the great cold bald hereafter ahead of her, so that as the child made her way across the muddy disconsolate river of death she would have a name, and so a history: *Rose,* she whispered again.

Rose. Her mother's name, she believed then and now and on to the end of all belief, the end of all time, the end of a history placed squarely on the backs of those worthy enough to bear it, those with the resolve to bear it.

Rose. Her mother's name, she believed, though she had never heard it spoken, never knew a name existed.

A Part of It

HE WAS IN HIS CAR, THREE DOORS DOWN AND ACROSS THE STREET from her house. He had the lights off, the engine running.

He gave her ten minutes more. That was all. He looked at the clock on the dash, then held up his watch to the light from the streetlamp, saw they were two minutes apart. He could not say which time was correct, whether the car clock was two minutes behind or if his wristwatch was two minutes ahead.

But that didn't matter. It was ten minutes that mattered. Only that.

He'd been out here a half hour already, waiting. This was one of her ploys, he knew. Get him here, a place where he ought not be, then make him wait.

He'd taken her call on the phone in the den, careful to catch it on the first ring. He'd held the receiver to his ear, heard nothing. Signal enough, he knew. Then, loud enough for his wife to hear, he said, "All right." Then, "Yep, tomorrow. So long."

Then he'd gone to the kitchen, opened the refrigerator, saw they needed milk.

"Going for milk," he called out to his wife. "Back in a few," he called out.

That was a half hour ago. There would be a story to give once he got home, always was. He'd gone out for milk or eggs or bread a dozen times at least in the last two months. Then, when he came home, he would give his wife the story. He would talk—he was good at that—and get his wife to believe the cataclysm, the car in a ditch he'd seen, traffic on Mathis Ferry Road tied up so bad he couldn't move for forty minutes, or the electricity gone out at the Harris Teeter, no one allowed to leave the market. He could talk.

He thought he saw movement inside the front window, thought he saw the shadow of a figure, and he moved in his seat, blinked.

He looked at the car clock, saw the pale red numbers turn from *10:17* to *10:18*, then held his wristwatch up again: *10:20*. Seven minutes left.

Then her front door opened, and light spilled from inside onto her yard and the narrow brick walkway.

There she was, silhouetted in the doorway, and he smiled at his resolve, as though giving her ten minutes had flushed her out.

She stepped onto the porch, and he saw then, behind her, her husband. He slipped lower in his seat.

Her husband followed her out, and the two turned, faced the house. He could see she had her hands on her hips, saw, too, her husband reach to the porch light fixture, a carriage lamp to the left of the door. He saw the husband's hands working.

Then came the flush of yellow light from the fixture, and he saw what they were doing: changing the bulb, and he wondered what she meant by this exchange, wondered what she wanted him to see in this act. He wondered what signal she was sending to him.

The husband stood back from the light and next to his wife. He put his arm around her, as though this endeavor were a triumph. *How many adulterers does it take to change a lightbulb?* he thought, and believed perhaps he had heard this joke before, that he wasn't making it up right then, watching her and her husband. But he could recall no punch line.

The husband let go of her, gave her a gentle push from behind so that she headed toward the open door first. From where he sat in the car he could see the husband give his wife the smallest pat on the bottom, saw her turn and smile up at him, say something. He could see her face, her smile, her hair, all of it bathed in the yellow light from the new bulb.

Then she was inside, gone.

The husband still stood on the porch, looking at the fixture, admiring his handiwork, his hands now on his hips, just as his wife had stood. He looked at the light.

Then the husband turned, looked straight at him.

Though he knew the husband could not see him, down here in the dark and inside the car, he tried to slip even lower in his seat, tried to disappear.

Still the husband looked at him, hands on his hips.

Then, slowly, the husband raised an arm, and waved.

He swallowed, felt his face go hot. He tried to slip even deeper down, tried to melt away, but there was nowhere for him to go.

The husband brought down his hand, stood with his hands on his hips once again. He looked at him a moment longer, then turned, stepped back inside. The door was closed, the husband gone.

A few seconds later the porch light went out.

He looked at the dash clock, saw the numbers: *10:19*.

All of this in one minute.

He sat up, careful not to hold his wristwatch to the light from the streetlamp, that movement suddenly flamboyant, extravagant, and put the car in reverse. He looked behind him, left the lights off, and backed down the block to the stop sign four houses down.

Only after he'd put the car into drive, turned, and headed away down East Hobcaw did he turn on the headlights.

He pushed the garage door opener on the visor, saw the door lift before him.

There stood his wife in the doorway from the garage into the kitchen, waiting.

She had on her bathrobe, her arms crossed, her face white from the headlights on her, behind her the light from the kitchen.

He eased in, cut off the lights. Now she was lit only with the pale light from the garage door opener, her features gone. He turned off the engine, opened his door. He felt himself smiling. His palms were wet, his face still hot.

He said, "You wouldn't believe what happened," and pushed closed the door. Only then did he realize he hadn't come up with the story yet, hadn't figured this one out. He'd only seen her face in yellow light, smiling up at her husband behind her, speaking to him. And he'd only seen her husband, had only seen his hand, waving to him the whole way home.

But he could talk. He knew that.

He shook his head, stopped the smile. He let out a silent whistle, shook his head again. He stood beside the car a moment, hands on his hips, then thought better of this stance, instead put his hands in his pockets. He started around the hood of the car and toward her, his shoulders up, as though the garage had suddenly gone cold.

"You're not going to believe what happened," he said.

She said, "The milk."

He stopped. He blinked, looked at her. He'd forgotten the milk.

Quickly he looked from her to the car, as though a gallon of milk in a Harris Teeter bag might miraculously appear on the front seat.

He took a breath, slowly turned back to her.

He said, "Well, that's part of it. That's a part of it." He paused. Though he wanted to give a gesture, wanted to shake his head yet again, let out another silent whistle, wanted, even, to put his hands on his hips, nothing came to him.

She looked at him, waiting. He could hear from behind him the tick of the engine, felt, too, the heat off it.

He said, "This whole thing is incredible. You're not going to believe what happened."

She turned, headed back into the kitchen.

Appraisal

"Mrs. Jensen," the appraiser said, and nodded, though his eyes wouldn't meet mine. I stood there with the front door open, the dog in the laundry room barking and whining. "I need to look around inside now," he said. "If it's okay."

"Sure," I said, and smiled. "Come on in. The dog's just a barker. She's a sweetie," I said, like I had to let him in on some secret it was only me to know.

But he wasn't here about the dog.

He nodded again, wiped his shoes on the welcome mat, his eyes still down. He couldn't have been more than twenty or twenty-one and had on a tie and shirt, a corduroy coat, khaki pants, and loafers. He'd been outside the house, poking around, videotaping, writing things down on the clipboard he carried.

He was here to appraise the house, something Ben and I knew was coming but hadn't really looked forward to. This was about the house, about how we were trying to get out from under all we'd been piling up for the last twenty-seven years.

Bankruptcy was the word, actually. Bankruptcy, and though Ben and I had seen on any number of videotapes the lawyer had us watch that the word *bankruptcy* wasn't anything to be ashamed of, that in fact it was something good, a way to start over and make your life back into something it'd been intended for, namely solvency, it was still a word I wouldn't use.

Twenty-seven years. Three kids, all grown and gone, the youngest, our Amber, no older than this boy here in our foyer, already away to college. And Ben and I starting over, like the lawyers on those videotapes were nothing other than people telling us how to put new vinyl siding up on our lives, like this was no more than me deciding to change my hairstyle, or Ben buying a convertible.

But this kid. This appraiser. He knew what this was about, I was certain. You didn't come out at the request of the courts and make an appraisal if the owners were moving on into a bigger house or getting transferred. No, he knew.

The video camera hung by a strap off one shoulder, one of those industrial tape measures in his hand, that clipboard in the other. He looked off to the left into the dining room, then to the right, into the living room, where until last week we'd had the piano. Fifty-two years in the family, and we'd gotten a thousand dollars for it from Patterson Music, included in the price two old men sent out to move it for free.

Last night while I lay in bed trying to fall asleep, Ben downstairs and watching TV like he does now until four or five in the morning, I'd done the math in my head, a kind of sheep counting that didn't do a thing for making me sleepy: fifty-two years into a thousand dollars was a little over nineteen dollars a year; three generations—my grandmother, my mother, me—into a thousand dollars was three hundred thirty-three dollars a generation.

One marriage into a thousand dollars was a thousand dollars. Money.

I said, "You want some coffee?" and turned, still smiling, for the kitchen.

"That'd be nice," he said. "If it's not too much trouble."

"This kind of trouble is nothing," I said. "Coffee is no trouble at all."

I knew he knew what this was all about.

He had the tape measure pulled out across the dining room floor when I came back in, two coffee cups in hand. I'd stopped at the laundry room door on the way out of the kitchen, whispered loud, "Missy, you hush!" to the dog, who hadn't yet given up her yelping. She's short-haired, splotched with black and white and brown and yellow, thirty-five pounds or so, and what I call Multiracial as a kind of joke when people ask what she is. "Multiracial," I say, my face all straight when I'm out in the neighborhood with her on the leash, and then I watch their faces, the faces of these people who've somehow, as best as I can figure, found solvency in their lives, though you can never be sure about that, about what happens inside all these nice polite homes just like mine. But I watch their faces as a means to judge whether or not they have a sense of humor, whether or not they can see through how thin and stupid words are once you try to make them something else.

Stone Broke into *Bankrupt* into *Starting Over*.

Occasionally they get the joke, smile, shake their heads. But mostly people only glance up at me real quick, just to make sure they've heard the right word, and then nod their heads sagely, understanding. Then they move along.

Still the dog barked in the laundry room.

"Here you go," I said, and handed him the cup. "Cream, no sugar, right?"

He looked up from his clipboard to the coffee cup, smiling as though the cup had made itself, presented itself to him of its own. "Exactly right," he said to the cup, and nodded, lifted it to his lips, winced at it. The cup was one we'd gotten up in Mount Pisgah National Forest, at the gift shop at the Forest Discovery center up there. Back when we had money and traveled. Before an heirloom piano had been turned magically into a thousand bucks.

When the cup's sitting on the shelf in the cupboard, it has a picture of Smokey Bear standing beside a green forest, waving. Only now, the coffee inside the cup, the forest was burned down, just crispy sticks; the joke of it is that when you pour hot liquids into the cup, the green disappears because of the heat, leaving behind the black burned-out picture beneath.

It seemed funny when we bought it, anyway.

But this kid didn't even look at the picture long enough to think about it, those woods burned down to nothing, dead. He only looked at his clipboard, scribbled on the form there, and set the cup on the dining room table, started reeling in the tape.

"I have to get measurements for the rest," he said, and nodded at the floor. He finished with the tape, turned and headed into the living room.

I sat on the staircase, my cup in my hands—this one had a picture of the state of Alaska on it, another trip we'd made—

and sipped. Ben was asleep upstairs in the guest r
he'd taken up residence the night after we met witl
for the first time, his clothes filling the closet up thei∪.

It's a childish thing, I know, him thinking that if he went in
there, slept away from me, stayed up late and let his job go to
hell in a handbasket that things might work their way out. Or
that it might get so bad something or someone would come to
rescue him. Like I was his mommy or something.

But, in all actuality, it's a nice arrangement: the entire closet
all to myself, and that whole California king, the bed an artifact
from the old days, when we were flush with money. When we
ate out like we had no kitchen, like we'd never bought china.
When we bought the kids every tape, CD, video, computer
game they even uttered the name of. Back when we went places,
Ben and me, alone: that cruise up the Alaskan shore, New Year's
in New York, Mardi Gras.

"Mrs. Jensen?" the boy called out from the kitchen, and I
stood from the stairs, went to the kitchen.

He stood with the tape in hand, a finger to the little handle
you turn to wheel it in. He nodded at the laundry room door,
where Missy was still yelping away, even louder now. "Is that
the laundry room?" he said.

"Yes," I said. His eyes were on my chin, as though if he were
given enough time in here he might actually graduate to eye
contact.

"I'll need to measure that, too." He shrugged. Maybe he was
looking at my mouth now, I couldn't say.

I shrugged, too. I'd have to put Missy out in the yard first.

"Maybe you should go on upstairs, take care of things up there while I put the dog out."

"Fine," he said, a little too quickly, and turned, headed around the counter and back to the stairs.

I turned, put my hand on the laundry room door. Missy was worked up now, and I thought of that word, *Multiracial,* and thought for a moment too on how people would look me in the eye one way or the other, to see if it was a joke or to signal me they understood the wisdom of avoiding the word *Mutt* in this day and age.

But then I heard the boy on the stairs and remembered Ben asleep in the guest room, and I thought maybe that would be nice, letting the boy walk in on him, wake him up. An appraiser looking in on my husband for a kind of appraisal of his life: going bankrupt and sleeping away his job. That might wake him up, I thought, in more ways than one: a stranger looking down on him in bed, appraising him.

"Excuse me!" I called out, trying to make my voice sound like a whisper and be loud enough to hear, like I didn't want him to wake anybody up. Which was a lie. I placed my coffee cup on the counter, called out "Excuse me!" again, and headed for the stairs.

He stood at the top, half turned, clipboard at the ready, the video camera still hung at his shoulder. I started up, smiling, and it seemed maybe he was looking at my nose now.

"My husband," I whispered. "Ben. He's asleep up here, so we'll need to be quiet."

He looked down at the clipboard, like it might speak to him.

"But I'll need to take a look," he said. He shrugged. "You know. To get the measurements. To take a look."

"Oh, that's fine," I said, and passed him. He took a step back, still with his eyes to the clipboard. "We'll just need to be quiet. He's having a tough time with all this. He's not sleeping well, not since we've filed . . ."

I let the words trail off, watching him to see if he knew the blank I'd left him to fill in. I was at the guest room door now, the first one on the left, my hand to the knob, just like it'd been for the laundry room a few seconds ago, and I could still hear Missy down there, yelping away.

Why wasn't Ben awake yet, I wondered for an instant, with Missy yelping like that?

But then the boy gave a hard nod, and finally he let his eyes meet mine. "Bankruptcy," he said. "I know." He shrugged, and his eyes went right back to the clipboard. "This is a difficult thing." He shrugged again.

He'd looked at me only that long: three words. But long enough to hand me a lie. He *didn't* know what this was like. He had no clue.

I thought for a moment about leaving the door shut, about ushering him downstairs and sending him on his way for lying to me like this. But here we were, solvency our aim. My husband about to be awakened from sleep.

I opened the door, stepped in.

There sat the bed, empty. Stripped to the mattress. Even the pillow was gone. The closet door stood halfway open, and I could see inside there a couple of empty hangers. Nothing else.

I looked at all this for a few seconds; looked at it, tried to take it in. To figure it out: an empty room.

But then I remembered I wasn't alone, and I looked behind me at the boy, then at the room, at the boy again. He stood in the doorway, his mouth open a bit, clipboard at the ready, and then he let his eyes meet mine again, but for even a shorter time. Not even long enough for a word.

But what could he have said? Or me?

He only went to the far wall, laid the end of the tape measure on the floor, started reeling it out, measuring.

Missy yelped.

I was still in the room, sitting on the mattress, when he finished with the rest of the upstairs. He stood out in the hall, looking at the clipboard, and said, "Mrs. Jensen, we need to get a look at that laundry room now."

I stood. The laundry room, I thought. What does that mean, the laundry room?

But then it came to me: my life, this house. Empty hangers, a barking dog.

I didn't even bother looking at him as I came out of the room, headed down the stairs. We had work to do. We had the laundry room.

And then I was in the kitchen, and I had hold of my coffee cup. I put my hands around it, took a sip: cold. But it didn't matter. Alaska didn't matter, and I wondered where in the house the appraiser's cup was, wondered if the forest had grown back now that the coffee had gone cold, and I saw Smokey Bear waving, saw a green forest, lush and alive.

Starting Over, I thought. *Bankrupt,* I thought.

I looked at him, dared him to look at me one more time. There were things I could tell him about difficulty he would never know, things I could tell him without opening my mouth, without letting out the kinds of things that made for betrayal: words. I could let him know it all with only my eyes.

But he wouldn't look at me. He only cleared his throat, glanced at his watch, adjusted the camera strap on his shoulder.

I opened the door, the appraiser a few feet behind me, tape measure ready.

Here was Missy, our Mutt. Our Bitch Mutt.

I let her go, and she made a beeline for the appraiser's leg.

So I'd lied about her being a barker. About her being a sweetie. Truth was, she'd bite you soon as look at you.

I looked at him, this boy. The appraiser. Missy was already latched on, her short hair bristled at the neck, black and white and brown and yellow fur all blurred with the way she shook her head, holding on.

The boy had that leg out in front of him like a dancer. He dropped the clipboard, the tape, even the video camera, all of them making loud noises in this empty house, the place a lot quieter now Missy'd stopped yelping.

"Help!" he said, first quiet, then again, louder. "Help!" He was looking at me as best he could, his eyes shooting from the dog to me, him dancing there in my kitchen, this boy trying to shake off my dog. But he was looking at me, his eyes into mine, finally.

"She's a sweetie," I said, testing the words, the lie of them.

"Get it off me!" he shouted now, his eyes pleading, or at

least the shard of them I could see when he wasn't looking at the dog. "Help!" he shouted, and now he was kicking full force, the dog holding on for dear life.

"Heirloom," I said, testing the truth this time. "A thousand bucks," I said.

Still he kicked, and now I picked up my coffee, sipped at it and winced, as though it were hot.

"Appraisal," I said, my eyes hard on him while still he danced, me waiting to see in his eyes a sense of humor about life, about all things, about the difficulty in living he'd told me he knew, and now I could see a little blossom of blood on his pant leg, there where Missy had hold of him, our sweetie holding on tighter and tighter.

I watched for whether or not he could see how thin and stupid words are once you try to make them something else. Or if he was like most every idiot who nodded sagely, as if he understood.

But his eyes were only pleading.

"Solvency," I said; then, "Bankrupt," and I waited.

THE ISSUE
OF MONEY

IT IS SO HOT CAROL AND LEE FINALLY DECIDE TO ABANDON THEIR apartment and check into a motel, both knowing full well they cannot afford it.

"It damn well better have air-conditioning at least," Lee calls to Carol while she is on the phone.

She puts her hand over the receiver. "Will you shut up? It does. And a swimming pool." She takes her hand off the phone and asks about prices.

She says to her husband, "Forty-nine dollars a night."

He does not turn from the couch, does not move in any way to signal her what to do. The baby is sitting on his lap, and Lee jiggles him to keep him from crying.

It is seven-thirty in the morning. They have been awake since four twenty-one with the baby. None of them could sleep in the heat.

"Lee?" Carol says, wanting an answer. I would do it, she thinks. I would pay one hundred dollars a night to get out of here. "Lee?"

"How long is this supposed to last?" he says. "The heat." They cannot afford even one night, he knows.

"Until day after tomorrow. That's two nights."

"Hell, let's do it," he says, resigned, as if the matter is no longer in his hands, is now her responsibility. Lee stops bouncing the baby for only a moment, and he cries. Dressed only in a diaper and T-shirt, the baby is already soaked from sweat. Lee gently blows on the boy, temporarily cooling him down and temporarily stopping the crying.

After Lee leaves for work, Carol begins packing a small suitcase for the three of them. Check-in time is noon, and she plans to be right there, the baby in one arm, the suitcase in the other. She tries to imagine what they will need, decides on swimsuits, shorts, two shirts apiece, and of course underwear. And her uniform for work the next day. And toiletries. And there's the baby's port-a-crib. And the baby bag, the baby seat, the formula. . . . She stops thinking of all she needs when she realizes it will probably take two or three trips to the car and back just to load all they will need for two nights.

She decides to try on her swimsuit, the one she wore two summers ago, before she was pregnant. She knows she will most likely not fit into it, and she is right: the suit, a purple maillot with white lilies all over, cuts in at her thighs, barely holds in her breasts. She stands before the dresser mirror, turning sideways, looking over her shoulder at her buttocks, then facing front and looking at what she thinks are her enormous breasts, bulging stomach, fat thighs. She takes off her swimsuit and stands before the mirror, naked. She knows she is not as fat as all that; still, there are stretch marks down her abdomen and around her hips, and small ones on the side of each breast. She sits on the edge of the bed, and cries.

At least I feel cooler with no clothes on, she thinks. The baby, in an infant seat on the floor, looks at her, cooing. She wipes tears away, picks up the baby, and goes to the kitchen for a glass of ice water.

The sky is a dusty yellow all day long, at least the small patch of it Lee can see out the window in his office. The radio announces that a smog alert has been issued for the valley, and Lee takes in a deep breath. The pain he feels is far down in his lungs, a dull ache signaling that indeed the air is full of dirt. He coughs, and goes back to his stack of purchase orders.

On the way home, he just misses rear-ending the car in front of him, traffic on the freeway stopping dead several times. He is preoccupied with the idea of the motel and pool and the air-conditioning. He takes his exit off the freeway and drives past his apartment complex. He smiles, thinking about the sweltering heat inside that small place.

It is freezing inside the motel office; goose bumps appear immediately on his arms and chest. He can feel his legs prickling against the inside of his pant legs, and he scratches at his calves.

He rings the service bell, and an elderly Vietnamese woman comes out from the inner office. She is dressed in a purple and gold paisley dashiki and black slacks and moves slowly, determinedly, as though her steps from the inner office are choreographed. She reminds him of one of those life-size mannequins that emerge from huge clocks in Germany, on the hour every hour, to chop down trees or to play trumpets or simply to bow or curtsy, then disappear until the next hour. Clocks he has seen on television.

She walks slowly to the front desk, pulls from a drawer a pen and register form, sets them on the desk. She turns the ledger around to him, picks up the pen, then looks at him.

"Name?" she says, though the inflection is barely present, and the question becomes for him a demand.

"Mason," he says. "Lee Mason. My wife is already here."

The woman looks down from him to the large ledger, turns it around to face her, and slowly moves a finger down the list of names. "Mason," she says. "Mason." Her finger stops. She smiles and looks up at him.

All her teeth are capped in gold, and he feels more goose bumps form, though he is not sure it is the temperature in here or this woman with gold teeth.

"Mason," she says again. "Mason, your wife leave you."

"What?" he says, shaking his head a little, as though he were hard of hearing.

She grins even more. "Mason, your wife leaving you. She come here. Baby, suitcase. She crying." The old woman slowly motions with her hands down her face, a graceful streaking of fingertips that, he supposes, represents his wife's tears.

"No," he says. "We're checking in to stay through this heat. Through this heat wave. I had to work today, so she had to check in herself."

The woman throws her head back quickly and lets out a long, high laugh, her whole body shaking. This move startles Lee, and it is in this moment he resolves to leave this motel, to get out of there with his wife and child as soon as he can and find another place to stay.

She stops laughing, and smiles, says, "Your wife leaving you, Mason. This heat never over. This heat never finish through. Good for business."

Lee says, "What room? What room is my wife in?"

She stops smiling, says, "Twelve A." She resumes her mechanized movement, putting the pen and form back in the drawer, turning the ledger around, walking the prescribed arc back into the inner office. Lee hears quick, high-pitched voices begin when the woman walks into the other room.

Carol is by the pool, the baby asleep in the port-a-crib next to her, a makeshift umbrella made from two clothes hangers and a beach towel protecting the baby from the sun. She is wearing an old pair of gym shorts and a blue T-shirt over her swimsuit; what little breeze there is cools her down.

She sees Lee coming down the walk, looking at doors. "Lee," she calls, and sits up in her lounge chair.

Lee turns to her voice. His face is almost white, his eyebrows raised, his mouth open. His shirt is sweated through around his neck, armpits, and chest. She stops waving, her hand in midair as if posing for a photograph. But she is not smiling.

Lee takes off his tie, and as he moves closer, Carol can see the sweat on his face. He wads up the tie in one hand and sits down in a chair next to Carol. She swallows, settles back in the lounge chair, and watches him. He is going to tell me he wrecked the car, she thinks. Or he is going to tell me he lost his job.

He says, "Look, we have to get out of this place. We can't afford it. I knew it from the beginning. We shouldn't have checked in here in the first place."

Is that all it is? Carol wonders. The money? She closes her eyes and puts her head back. "I can work up some extra time tomorrow. I don't mind."

"And that woman," Lee says, not listening. "That Vietnamese woman in there is crazy. She thinks you and I are split up. She thinks the reason you came in here is because you left me." He wipes his forehead with his tie.

She laughs, still keeping her eyes closed. If she can disregard his pleading long enough, he will give in, she thinks. "Oh, that," she says. "I was sniffling a little bit when I came in. She thought I was crying, and I told her it was just the air. The smog."

Lee sits hunched over, his hands between his knees. He looks at the ground, then says, "That old lady scares the hell out of me. I don't even like being around this place, knowing she's here."

Carol looks up at him. "Lee," she says, meaning, *Don't be ridiculous.* "What you need is to go lay out in the room for a while, then put your trunks on and go swimming. That's what we did." She points to the baby, still asleep under the towel. "We took a little nap, then went swimming. You go down there and take a nap. Here's the keys." She reaches into her purse and flips him the keys. He fumbles them, dropping them on the cement. She laughs.

As he heads for the room, Lee stops and turns back to Carol, noticing for the first time the gym shorts and T-shirt. "What are you wearing?" he says.

She pretends she does not hear him, and closes her eyes.

. . .

Carol is right; the nap does him good. Though he does not like how ugly the room is—a hot plate sitting on a nightstand is chained to the floor, pictures of wide-eyed hoboes decorate the walls, and the carpeting is a dull orange—he is thankful it is cool and quiet inside and feels refreshed after sleeping a half hour, sprawled across the bed in his underwear.

The world is new to him when he comes out of the room. It is dusk, and the sky is a brilliant red. He forgets for a moment that the color is due to the smog, and wonders at the beauty of this early evening.

Carol and the baby are in the pool, Carol laughing, holding the naked boy, walking his feet along the water.

"Feel better?" Carol says, looking up from the baby.

He thinks they can probably afford to go to Bob's Big Boy for dinner, though he wishes they could go anywhere in the world, anywhere so long as it is not the kitchen back in the apartment. "Fine," he says. "Great," he says, and dives in.

Carol wakes up after midnight, the baby screaming. The baby, in the port-a-crib next to the bed, gasps every few seconds, catching his breath. She turns the lamp on, pulls the cover back. The room is freezing. The baby's arms are cold, as are his feet and back. She picks him up and climbs back in bed, pulling the blanket and sheet over them both.

"Lee," she says, "Lee, wake up. It's freezing in here."

Lee is already awake but pretends he is asleep, opening his eyes only after Carol shoves him. "What?" he says. "What's wrong?"

"It's cold in here, that's what's wrong," she says. "Go over and turn off the air conditioner."

Lee slowly sits up and swings his legs over the edge of the bed. The room is ice-cold, and he imagines he can see his breath. He rubs his hands up and down his arms, stands, and goes to the air conditioner.

But he cannot find any way to turn it off, any sort of temperature control switch. The air conditioner is only a large brown box stuck in the window, cold air pouring out into the room. He cannot even find an electrical cord he can unplug.

"Call the front desk," Carol says to his back. Lee stands in his underwear, staring at the air conditioner, his arms around himself. He does not move.

He says, "Call up there yourself, you like that old woman so much."

"I will," she says.

She lets it ring four times, seven times, twelve times before hanging up.

"No answer."

"I suppose now you want me to go up there and knock on the door," Lee says. He turns around. Carol is silhouetted by the lamp on the nightstand. He sees her profile, but then she turns to him, and he loses her face in the dark. "Right?"

But there is no one at the front desk either. Lee bangs on the door, waits, bangs again. He puts his face to the window, cups his hands around his eyes, but the office is dark. He has on only a pair of shorts, and feels sweat trickle down his chest and the small of his back. He bangs on the door again, waits, then leaves.

He sits on a lounge chair by the pool, looking at the night sky.

The moon is brown through the smog and the temperature is only a few degrees cooler than during the day, but the darkness makes all the difference. In the darkness he cannot see everything.

He wonders how they will pay for the motel room for two nights, and how the air-conditioning in the room really works, what kind of wiring the contractors had done when they built the place. He wonders about new jobs, about money, about Carol. Mostly, he wonders what will happen. He wonders what will happen with the three of them, and has no answer.

Then Carol is standing next to him, silent, wearing the T-shirt and gym shorts. He looks from the moon to her. The baby is on her hip, asleep.

He likes it out here, Carol thinks. He likes being out here in this heat.

"Let's go for a swim," he says.

"Okay."

The pool is dark, and Lee quietly slips in. Carol places the baby in the middle of a lounge chair, then steps into the pool. When she is waist deep, she takes off her T-shirt and shorts, then slips out of her underwear. She tosses her wet clothes onto the cement, then swims to Lee, who is taking off his shorts. He tosses his clothes onto the cement, too, and they swim back and forth across the pool.

"I fixed the air conditioner," Carol whispers. "I kicked hell out of it, and I guess the control switch turned down a few notches. Anyway, it's a lot nicer in there." While she says this, though, she thinks, I do not want to go back in there. I want to stay out here. I want to swim.

Lee stops and stands up in the water. The water is chest-high, and Carol curls around him. They begin making love, the two of them there in the water, in the cool.

Lee opens his eyes, and the Vietnamese woman is standing at the edge of the pool. He thinks first it is his imagination, that this woman's image has come to haunt him, but then he blinks, and knows she is real. He quickly pulls away from Carol, who wonders what it is, what she has done to him. Is it me? she wonders. Me?

The woman laughs the same laugh she gave earlier, when Lee had come into the office. She says, "No swim after ten. I give you ten minutes for getting out, then you go back your room." She shakes her head, turns, and starts away. But then she stops, turns back to them, and says, "No, I give you half hour. Half hour for Masons." She laughs again. As she walks away, she says, "This heat wave never end. This heat last forever. This heat go on and on."

A few moments later, Carol turns back to Lee, who has not moved. He watches the woman move away.

"Lee," she says, "Lee, how much money do we have?"

He does not answer.

She puts her arms around his neck, and says, "How much longer can we stay here? How many more nights? I want to take off work tomorrow and just swim all day."

Lee looks at Carol. He can see her face in the light from the brown moon. Even in the pool he can feel the sweat trickling down his back, mixing with the water.

Carol is crying, and Lee does not know. To him, the tears are only water running down her face, water from the pool.

"Lee?" she says.

Nostalgia

SUMMER SUNDAY MORNINGS WE WENT TO THE BEACH. MOTHER and Dad heaped blankets and quilts over Brad and me in the cold bed of our green Dodge pickup. On our backs in the pickup bed, our eyes to the gray morning sky, I thought: I am tall. Lying on my back, my feet and the top of my head touched the side walls of the pickup bed, but I remembered Brad's knees were already bent. His head and feet touched both sides a year ago.

We rode in the pickup down Beach Boulevard while the fog lifted and cool air flapped the corners of the quilts; past the empty Hwy 39 Drive-In and down to Huntington Beach, the sand a half-mile wide and already warm. For lunch we sat in the sun and ate fried chicken cooked the night before.

Riding back evenings, sweatshirts on, hoods drawn tight around our faces and tied off in perfect Mother-bows, we passed a movie at the drive-in, *Mary Poppins* the whole summer long. We didn't speak, never spoke, until the screen ducked behind trees and disappeared.

Weekdays we laughed while folding newspapers we were to deliver, pulling rubber bands taut and shooting them; laughed reading headlines, not understanding what news was, what a box in the bottom corner of the front page meant listing something called Casualties: LtCol, SSgt, PFC and more PFCs. We didn't know what they meant.

. . .

One Saturday night, Mother and Dad went out. Dad sat in the living room in his peggers and penguin shirt and watched television, Mother in the bedroom in front of the mirror, still in bra and slip. The smell of cologne hung in the air. To me it was not unpleasant but was just Mother's smell.

"Charlotte will be here in a minute, boys," she said. She held a clear plastic mask in front of her face and sprayed her hair with another smell.

Brad and I sat on the edge of the bed, watching her reflection in the mirror. Brad said, "Mom, we don't need a babysitter. We're too old."

"Yeah," I said.

"I want you boys to behave tonight. She complained last time about you boys not behaving."

Brad turned to me and rolled his eyes. He hopped off the bed and left.

"We will," I said.

Mother sprayed deodorant. I picked up the plastic mask, held it to my face. I looked in the mirror.

"Don't play with that," Mother said, and took it from me.

Charlotte came to the front door a few minutes later, having walked from her house four doors up the street. She was old, in high school, and wore a red scarf over soupcan-size curlers, a man's white shirt untucked with the sleeves rolled up, black stretch pants with stirrups, and huarache sandals. Brad said she wasn't pretty. I didn't think so either. She had her own smell, but not as thick as Mother's.

Mother came out from the bedroom, zipped up the hip of her skirt, and instructed Charlotte: "Put them to bed at nine-thirty. No later. They can have some pop and chips, but not too much. They've already had dinner. Bed at nine-thirty." She turned to us. "You boys are on your best behavior. Kiss me goodbye. Brad." He gave her a reluctant peck on the cheek. "Richard." I did the same.

Daylight savings time, for a reason we could never figure, made the days longer. We could still play 500 in the street, find an ice-cream man somewhere in the tract, ride bikes to the playground and swing, swing high, and drop from the sky to the sand. But when Mother and Dad went out, we had to stay home.

On those nights we would stand in the front yard, kick off our thongs and look to the sky, then spin in circles, arms out to either side, until we fell like dead tops to the ground and watched the street, the world, spin around us, and felt our stomachs do somersaults.

Or we were in the backyard with our G.I. Joes, army men dressed in fatigues and black plastic army boots. We had a jeep for them, a truck, a cannon, guns, rations, ammo, more fatigues and boots. In the backyard was a pine tree, low and spreading. G.I. Joes would climb the tree to scout Russian territory. We dug dirt out from under some of the roots of the tree and built a command post, an ammo dump, a garage for the jeep.

G.I. Joes were always getting shot. Brad would put a G.I. Joe on the highest branch he could reach, and we would sit and throw pebbles and sticks until one of us knocked the doll down. The better the fall, the happier we were. If it got hung up in a branch, twirled its way down and around, and struck its head on the ground, we laughed.

Or we were in Dad's garden, the side yard between the Petersons' fence and our garage. Cherry tomatoes were all Dad grew, and in the early summer the plants crawled with tomato worms. Brad would get the lawn mower gas can and fill a jar, drop worms in, pull them out, and light them. They glowed and rolled like snake fireworks on Fourth of July afternoon sidewalks. We laughed at this, too.

"Don't go out of the backyard," Charlotte said this night, as soon as Mother and Dad had closed the door behind them.

"Don't worry," Brad said.

"Yeah," I said.

We went to the backyard and straight to the garden, ignoring the G.I. Joes. The tomato worms had all been gone some time; where they went we never knew.

But there were tomatoes. Dozens. Hundreds. Brad sent me in to get a paper bag from the kitchen. Charlotte, seated on the sofa and watching television, asked, "What do you want that bag for?" She didn't move her eyes from the set.

"To pick tomatoes," I said.

"Okay," she said.

We filled the bag with tomatoes. "Why are we picking so many?" I asked.

"Because," Brad said.

"Oh," I said, and picked.

After we'd filled the bag, Brad led us into the garage from the back door into the garden. Mother kept sweet things in the refrigerator in the garage—Fudgsicles, Popsicles, watermelon, Kool Pops—tempting us both all summer long. Back from the playground on hot summer afternoons, we went inside to the cool dark of the garage. Brad and I would open the refrigerator, take a Fudgsicle apiece, and swallow it whole.

One time Mother came from inside the house, apron on, plaid shorts to mid-thigh. "Are you still hungry? Still hungry?" she said. "I fed you two lunch not two hours ago. And you're still hungry? I'll teach you to be still hungry." She didn't have the Mother smell of Saturday nights, but instead smelled of oil and lemon and ammonia. "I'll teach you hungry. Every day I come out here and find two or four or eight less Popsicles. You're still hungry? Come with me."

She grabbed our wrists, Brad on one side, me the other, pulled us to the backyard, and sat us down on plastic lattice patio chairs. "You don't move," she said. She went back to the garage and brought back every box of ice cream, every Popsicle, the watermelon, Kool Pops. "You will eat all of this. Now. Start."

We ate, pretending we were hurt and sick and sorry; ate all the ice cream, spit out every seed, sucked all color from the frozen ices, and smiled and laughed when Mother didn't see.

That night at dinner we were silent. "Your sons ate all the desserts in the house," Mother said to Dad. "I made them. They were stealing ice creams and things out of the refrigerator in the garage when I told them not to."

"You boys," Dad said.

Brad and I pretended we were hurt and sick and sorry, and kicked each other's legs beneath the table.

On this night, though, the freezer was empty save for a bag of ice and five pounds of ground beef. We went back to the garden, to the backyard, and brought the tomatoes inside. Brad put the bag on the camel saddle at the foot of his bed. Charlotte hadn't seen us bring them in.

"What are you doing in there?" she called from the living room.

"Nothing," Brad yelled back.

"Nothing," I said too.

Brad turned to me. "Watch," he said. We went from the bedroom to the kitchen, Brad leading, and out to the backyard.

"Where are you boys going?" Charlotte called again, without looking up from the television.

"Out back," Brad said.

"Yeah," I said.

"Okay."

But instead we went to the front yard, Brad tall enough to unlock the gate. I closed the gate behind me. "Why are we out here?" I asked. "We just told Charlotte we were going to be in the back."

"Because we want to."

"Oh."

There were no neighbor kids around, so we stood in the front yard and spun, arms out like helicopter blades, eyes to the spinning sky. I fell first, Brad a few spins later. We laughed.

I was panting, trying to get my breath back. "Charlotte—don't—know—we're—out—here?"

"Yeah." Brad was out of breath, too.

"Should we go back into the backyard?"

"No. We're out here. She doesn't care. She's ugly." His breath was coming back.

"Yeah," I said. "She doesn't care."

We lay there on the ground a few minutes, letting ourselves breathe easier and our stomachs settle down. Then Brad got up from the grass and went to the garage door, tried to lift it but could not.

"What are you doing?" I rolled my head over on the grass until I faced him. My head was still on the ground so that Brad and the driveway and the house were all sideways.

"Help me," Brad said.

I rolled over and got up. We both pushed the garage door, but could only get it three-quarters open. Brad froze, hands up to catch the door if it fell, but only stood there a moment. "Let's get our bikes," he said. He dropped his hands from the door and went in.

"Huh?"

He was already in the garage with his hands on his bike, his foot toeing up the kickstand. I took two slow steps for my bike.

The front screen door opened and banged against the side of the house. Charlotte came toward us, her fists clenched.

"Listen, you little bastards. I'm not going to put up with any more crap from you two. You punks don't think I can hear a garage door opening? Get back in the house."

She took my wrist and moved toward Brad.

Brad slowly put down the kickstand, put his hands in his pockets, and started off for the house. Charlotte tried grabbing

his wrist, but Brad shook her off, looked at her through eyes
half closed, lips thin, straight.

"I'm going," he said.

Charlotte hesitated a moment, then said, "Well you damn
well better be." She gripped my wrist tighter. "I'm telling your
parents!" she yelled.

Brad was already on the porch and pulled the screen door
open with one hand, the other still in his pocket.

Charlotte half pulled me into the house. "You bastards," she
said again as she pushed me into our bedroom. "Don't even try
coming out of this room until I say so." She slammed the door,
bouncing our framed cowboy and Indian pictures against the
wall.

"I don't care," Brad said. He stood up from the bed and
looked out the window onto the front lawn.

"We're going to get a whipping," I said. "She's going to tell
Dad and Mother, and we're going to get a whipping." I started
crying then, hissing air out and taking quick breaths in.

"Oh, shut up, you wimp." Brad stared out the window. "I'm
too old for a babysitter. You should be too."

He looked out the window a few seconds longer, then blinked,
turned from the window. He looked at the bag of tomatoes on
the camel saddle and blinked again.

Then he picked it up, opened the door, and went out into the
hall. He didn't even look at me.

But I followed him, wiping tears from my eyes with the palm
of one hand. He stopped in the living room. Charlotte sat on the
couch and faced the television, her back to us.

"We're going," Brad said.

I didn't say anything.

Charlotte jumped. She turned her head around, her eyes already slits, her lips pursed. She stood up slowly from the couch. "Going where?"

"Outside." Brad put his hand inside the bag of tomatoes.

Charlotte came slowly around the edge of the couch. "You get back to your room. Now." She shot her arm out as though it were a bayonet pointed toward our room. "Now!"

Brad pulled a tomato out of the bag and cocked his arm back. "Don't touch me."

She put her hands on her hips. "You going to throw that at me? Huh?" she said, and cocked her head to one side. "I dare you," she said. She took a step closer. "Come on, I dare you." She stopped. "Twerp."

Brad hesitated a moment, then threw the tomato.

It hit her shoulder and burst open on the white shirt. Charlotte stood looking at her shirt, then at us. She took a step backward.

There was nothing she could do, so I threw tomatoes then, too.

We emptied the bag, backed Charlotte into a corner of the kitchen until her white shirt was covered with seeds, skins, and tomato juice. We ran out of the house and into the garage, rode to the playground, and stayed there until dark.

When we came home Charlotte was on the couch, the television still on. Her shirt was still dirty, but she had managed to get most of the seeds and skins off. She didn't say a word.

Brad stood before her in the middle of the living room. "We're going to stay up," he said.

"Yeah," I said.

We sat down two feet from the set and watched television.

And later heard the car outside. As though on cue we three jumped up, Brad and I running to the bedroom, Charlotte out the front door. We couldn't hear what she said to Mother, but watched from our darkened room as she waved her arms, pointed to her shirt, and shook her finger in Mother's face. Charlotte left for home without letting Dad pay her.

I started crying again. "What do we do now?" I said. Through wet eyes I saw a tear drip down Brad's face to the corner of his mouth and in.

"Shut up," he said. "Stop crying. I don't know."

Then Mother stood in the bedroom doorway, only a silhouette in front of the hall light. "What the hell do you think you're doing? Can't we even go out once in a while without you tearing down the house and terrorizing the babysitter? Your father. Your father will give you a whipping for this." She slammed the bedroom door closed. Again the pictures bounced.

A few seconds later the door opened slowly and Dad appeared, silhouetted as Mother had been. My crying was loud now, blubbering. Brad was crying, too, but silently.

"You boys," he said.

He looked at us a few minutes in the light cast from the hall, then left. That was all.

We did not have Charlotte for a babysitter again.

2

"Should we bring the boys?" Mother said at dinner a month later.

"Sure," Dad said. "Good for them."

"What do you mean, good for them? A funeral?"

"Why did you ask me?"

"All right, they'll go."

"Who's the funeral for?" Brad asked.

"A funeral?" I said.

Mother gave me another helping of peas. "Eat this. Mrs. Fitzweld's son Ronnie. Charlotte's brother."

Charlotte's brother. He was real old. He graduated from high school. He was in the army.

Brad put both elbows on the table and put his chin in his hands. "What happened? Did he get killed?"

"Never mind. Get your elbows off the table."

"Aw, come on."

"That's enough." She stared at Brad until he took his elbows off the table and finished eating.

The funeral was up in the hills of San Pedro at a cemetery looking out over the Pacific. It seemed we would never get there. Brad leaned forward and crossed his arms over the top of the front seat between Mother and Dad. "Why are we all going so slow? The people behind us have their lights on, too. Why?"

I looked out the back window. They had their lights on, and it was daytime, the middle of summer.

"Because we're supposed to," Mother said. "This is a funeral procession."

I leaned forward and crossed my arms over the seat like Brad did. Dad looked at us in the rearview mirror. "You boys sit back," he said.

I sat back first, Brad a few seconds later.

"I was talking to Ricky Kohler about Ronnie," Brad said. "You know what, Mom? He says Ronnie was over in Viet Nam, and you know what else? He said Ronnie stepped on a land mind."

"That's enough."

"A land mind," Brad repeated. "How cool."

"Neat," I said.

At the service we sat in the back with the rest of the families on the block. Ricky Kohler sat next to Brad. Ricky was short and talked fast, a lock of hair always falling down in his eyes.

"Yeah," Ricky said, "a land mine. That's what my dad told me. He knows Mr. Fitzweld real good. They went over to the Pussy Willow the other night after Mr. Fitzweld found out about Ronnie." He pushed the lock of hair back into place. "My dad was real drunk when they got back from there. He forgot his keys and was knocking on my window when he got home. Mom would've killed him if she caught him coming home like that, but she was over at my aunt's house that night. So when I was—"

"You don't have to have a babysitter?" Brad cut in.

"No," Ricky said. "That's for babies." He pushed the hair up again. "You guys don't have a babysitter, do you?"

"No," Brad said quickly, and looked at me. I said nothing.

"So anyway," Ricky went on, "when I was helping him to bed I asked him what happened and he told me. He probably don't even remember." He laughed.

Mother, in the row in front of us, whispered over her shoulder, "You boys be quiet."

Ricky leaned over closer to Brad and whispered, "Yeah, and the weird thing is, Mrs. Fitzweld don't believe Ronnie's dead. Mr. Fitzweld told my dad it's because Ronnie got blown up, and they don't want nobody looking at his blown-up body, but Mrs. Fitzweld don't believe it. They wouldn't even open up the coffin for her to see him, he's so blown up."

Afterwards we all went outside into the hot summer morning for the burial. All I could see were a few soldiers and someone holding a brown umbrella over a few people seated next to the grave. We children were back behind most of the people there and only stood in silence, sweating.

I did not see Charlotte until later that day at the Fitzwelds' house. The house was full of neighbors, all the children playing outside in the yard. Mother came from inside onto the porch and called Brad and me in to see the Fitzwelds, but Brad wouldn't go, went instead across the street to the Adkins' front lawn and a football there.

Mother grabbed me by the wrist before I could follow Brad and pulled me into the house. I waded between people's waists until Mother finally broke through the crowd and I was standing in front of Charlotte and Mr. and Mrs. Fitzweld. Mother said something to them, but I just looked at Charlotte. She was crying into a handkerchief and was wearing a white blouse with pearl buttons, a gray skirt, and burgundy high heels. Her hair was a soft amber in a bouffant style, high on the top, curled under on the sides and back. All I could think about were those tomatoes breaking up on that old white shirt she wore and the tomato seeds and skins.

Charlotte looked up from her handkerchief at me, then whispered, "You bastard," just loud enough so that, with all the people talking everywhere, I was the only one who heard.

Her eyes were on me, digging into me and tearing at me. That was what I saw, and what I knew, and I knew I was alone too, in the Fitzwelds' living room, in the middle of a hundred thousand people. A million people. In the middle of everyone, dead and alive.

That was what I saw, and what I knew.

She started crying into the handkerchief again, and Mother pulled me away from Charlotte and back into the crowd, saying something about staring and being polite.

Mother and Dad stayed in the house, but I went back outside and walked home. The gate to the backyard was open. Brad was already in the backyard under the pine tree playing with G.I. Joes.

"Watch this," he said as I closed the gate behind me.

He dug a hole in the sand and put his hand in it, palm up. Then he buried it with the other hand and walked a G.I. Joe over the area. "Land mind!" he shouted, and brought the buried hand straight up into the air, flipping the doll end over end until it landed on its head in the sand. Brad laughed.

I laughed, too, though I thought I probably shouldn't.

I went inside.

A Way
Through This

HE BELIEVED THERE WAS A WAY THROUGH THIS. HE BELIEVED IT with all his heart.

He said, "I can see us getting through this."

She said nothing. She set her coffee cup on the table, looked out the kitchen window onto the small backyard. She saw the three trees back there, the sandbox he'd built, an old swing set. Past it all stood a chain-link fence.

She thought then of the children, and of them playing on the swing set. They'd bought the swing set from a family down the street who'd bought for their own children a wooden play structure, complete with two towers, a rope ladder, a slide. There was a name for these structures, she knew.

Then she remembered her own children shouting in the car one afternoon as they passed 84 Lumber. "Look!" they'd shouted. "Pirate's Fortress! Pirate's Fortress!" She'd turned, saw set up in the lumberyard parking lot the same wooden structure as in their neighbors' yard, a Pirate's Fortress, strung about it colorful pennants that reminded her of a used-car lot.

She believed there was no way through this. She believed it with all her heart.

He sat across from her at the table, had a can of Diet Coke instead of coffee. He brought the can to his lips, saw his hand begin to quiver. He allowed himself only a sip, thought perhaps the quivering was due to caffeine in the soda.

He thought then of his children, and of what they might think. He'd been the one to see them off this morning, his wife here at the table.

He'd smiled, the can of soda in his hand, and waved as they left for the bus at the end of the driveway. He'd seen Tina glance at him as she climbed up the steps and inside. Sam hadn't looked.

He wondered, now, what they might believe about their parents, about himself. He wondered if they knew he and his wife had not gone to bed last night but had stayed right here in the kitchen. He wondered if they knew they were trying to find a way through this.

He looked at her, still looking out the window.

He longed to look out the window with her, but would not allow himself that luxury: light, sky, green.

Instead, he looked only at the inside of this room, the kitchen. There was the toaster with its calico cover, the coffeemaker, the huge empty eye of the oven door, the refrigerator like a stone coffin on end.

He took up the soda again. Still his hand shook. This time, though, he knew it was not the caffeine but what he had done to bring them to this point in their lives.

What he had done.

She looked out the window, saw out there the world, and longed to be out there, floating free, maybe, above their house, above their backyard with its sandbox and swing set and chain-link fence, longed maybe even to be flying past this city toward some other place, some other home in a town she'd never visited, a home with no sandbox, a Pirate's Fortress instead of a swing set, her children there with her, all three of them playing in a lush and fenceless backyard; though she longed for all this, longed for it all in just these moments, there arose unbidden in her the image of her husband and the woman, so that suddenly she no longer flew above an unknown town, no longer even floated free above her own house and yard and sandbox and swing set, but was here, in the kitchen, a coffee cup before her, her husband across the table.

He took a sip of the soda. Still his hand quivered.

He looked around. He was still there in the kitchen of the home he and his wife owned. He saw the cupboards and the cabinets, the row of drawers beside the stove.

But now he could see inside the cabinets and cupboards the orderly rows in which his wife had placed their plates and glasses and pots and pans. He saw silverware in the top drawer beside the stove, saw hot pads and books of Green Back stamps in the drawer beneath that one. He saw, too, food his wife had purchased inside the refrigerator, saw more food inside the pantry, spices on the lazy Susan, lunch bags, and canisters full of flour and sugar and coffee.

He thought it a miraculous thing that he could see all this, the contents of their kitchen revealed to him like some secret out of his own life.

He looked at his wife, saw she still looked out the window.

He saw the two of them before all this, saw them making love in an innocent room, their own bedroom upstairs in this house, their home. He saw her above him, her eyes closed as she moved. He saw her beneath him, felt her arms around his neck as he moved.

It was his wife he saw, not the woman, and he believed this, too, to be a miraculous thing: the fact the pictures in his head were of himself and his wife, no one else. Though at times, he reasoned, the woman and what they had done would come to him now and again. Of course it would. How could it not?

But not here. Not now.

He could see everything in the kitchen. He could see the two of them—himself and his wife, not the woman—making love as they had before. He could see all of this.

"There's a way through this," he said. He took up the soda again. "I can see it," he said.

She heard in his voice his belief that there was a way. She could hear that he believed this with all his heart.

But with his words, too, in their pitch and conviction, she saw once again a Pirate's Fortress, saw again a lush and fenceless yard in a town she could not name. She saw her children, Sam and Tina. They were playing, all three of them pirates. Shipmates. They lived in a town she hadn't yet visited.

She said, "I see it." She picked up her cup, sipped at it. "You're right," she said. She said, "I can see us getting through this."

She turned to him, seated across from her at the table. She smiled at him.

He smiled, astonished at his luck, at the blessing of a wife who could see alongside him the way through this.

He allowed himself to look out the window then, a reward for his having hung on here, through this night. He saw an old swing set back there, saw a sandbox, too. He saw some trees, past it all a chain-link fence.

And above everything hung a bright and huge morning sky, a brilliant sky filled with limitless possibilities.

She looked from her smiling husband to the kitchen. Their children's breakfast dishes lay on the counter, ready to rinse for the dishwasher; the carton of orange juice sat beside the toaster, waiting to be put back in the refrigerator. There was the paraphernalia, too, she'd left out after making the children's lunches: a jar of mayonnaise and one of mustard, the plastic wrappers from slices of cheese, what was left of a bunch of grapes. An open bag of pecan sandies.

Evidence, she saw, of her shipmates, beloved cohorts in a Pirate's Fortress, and now the room became for her filled with limitless possibilities, the ceiling in here as broad and bright as the morning sky outside this window.

Still he smiled at her from across the table, but it seemed somehow her eyes were different now, and he saw in that moment the woman's eyes, saw in his wife's strange smile the pale pink of the woman's lips.

He blinked, felt terrible for this fleeting breach of her newfound trust in him and his belief that there was a way through this.

He blinked again, and here was his wife, the same eyes he loved, her same lips.

She looked back to her husband, but she could not see him.

He was gone, vanished into thin air, and she smiled, astonished at her luck, at the blessing of a husband who knew when to leave.

Even though he was afraid she might see how his hand quivered with the caffeine from sodas all night long, he reached to her then, moved his hand across the table toward her.

But he could not see his hand, nor could he see his arm. He looked down at himself, saw nothing, saw he had vanished into thin air, though he'd had no intention of ever leaving.

He had believed there was a way through this, had believed it with all his heart.

Then she stood from the empty table, turned to the kitchen counter, to the tidying up of everything before the children got home.

An Evening
on the Cusp of
the Apocalypse

THE MAIL HADN'T COME.

Larry'd put the bills—the electric, water, Citibank, the mortgage—in the mailbox when he left this morning, then pushed up the red flag and headed for downtown, confident in the way things worked: he would offer up these sacrifices, these slabs off his paycheck, in order to live as he and his family did, content in the good knowledge the lights were sure to come on when he flipped the switch, the water to flow when he turned on the faucet. Soon, he'd thought, as he placed the bills in the box, a representative from the United States Postal Service would arrive, take up these obligations, and send them on their way, route them as they ought to be routed, deliver as they ought to be delivered. The way things worked.

But the flag was still up, he saw in his headlights, this day over, the sun already down, dusk making way for dark, and he only shook his head at the sad truth of how seldom, in fact, things actually worked as they were meant to work. He pulled up in the driveway.

Take, for example, the library bid. He'd had this one in the bag, he'd believed, had done his homework, followed the paper trail first to the federal building, then to county, then to city, all in an effort to find exactly who it was could authorize the wiring bid. Routine, certainly: Be pleasant to Laqueesha, the black woman who worked the archives at federal, offer to buy her a cup of coffee and a jelly-filled, let her turn him down twice before trying one more time, when she always took him up on it; offer Dorinda at county a Snapple Raspberry Iced Tea, who would take it on the first go-round; make certain not to make eye contact with Benny O'Hearn, the bastard, down to city hall.

It'd paid off, too: the bid on the new library, he'd finally figured out, had to go through county, but not before approval by federal and by city.

Routine.

But then he'd gotten the flat tire, then the ticket for speeding, then, once he'd finally made it back to the office a little after five, he'd watched from his desk while a uniformed officer served papers to the boss, who turned, papers in hand, and went into his own office, closed the door gently behind him. A few moments later he emerged, briefcase in one hand, softball trophy in the other, and headed for the door.

Of course this would be about the death of that janitor at Whitesides Elementary last week, the one who'd touched wires he should have been able to touch.

They watched their boss go, no one saying anything, all nine of them at the offices of Hemley Electric, Inc., only staring as the door closed behind Mr. Hemley.

Then, one by one, they left, no words between them.

So much for the library bid.

Now he was home, the red flag still up, the bills not mailed. What next? he thought, and reached to the visor, pushed the button on the garage door opener.

Nothing happened.

He saw, too, there were no lights on in any of the windows, and his home, here in the failing twilight of a day gone bad, seemed somehow not his home at all but a hulking shadow, big and anonymous, nothing he knew as his own. It was a house, he saw, dark and vaguely empty for the lack of lights and a garage door shut tight, no matter how many times he mashed the button on the visor.

Was this his house? he wondered. Had he mistaken this one for his own, where each evening warm light through windows spilled softly onto the sidewalk and lawn and driveway? Maybe, he thought, he'd simply skipped a street, too preoccupied with the ramifications of that janitor's death and the ensuing fire that'd razed the entire elementary school the day before classes started, all of it simply cutting too close; it had been his schematic, after all, that'd been used for the layout and hookup, though his boss had given him the final verbal okay. He'd approached Mr. Hemley with the layout, sketched out on a Burger King napkin, between the top and bottom of the ninth inning of the last game of the season. Mr. Hemley'd just finished off his sixth beer and was headed for the on-deck circle when Larry'd made the presentation; Mr. Hemley'd smiled, nodded, then gone to bat, knocked a solid line drive down the first base line, drove in the winning two runs. Game over, schematic okayed. The world a wonderful place, Larry recalled. The way things worked.

But then had come that janitor, that fire. Maybe, Larry figured, he'd just made a left turn one street too early or one street too late, in this tract of homes. Maybe this house was just some-body else's, a simple mistake.

Then the garage door opened, not from the button—he'd finally given up, had in fact placed the car in reverse, so con-vinced he was of his error—to reveal to him his son, Lawrence, there in his headlights.

His thirteen-year-old was pushing up the garage door from the inside, grimacing with the effort, the red emergency release handle from the opening device dangling above him once he'd gotten the door all the way up.

"Hey, Dad!" he said, and waved, then stood to one side, made a sweeping gesture to usher him into the garage.

Larry smiled, pulled in, parked.

"How goes it?" Larry said, and climbed out. "What's with the garage door opener?" he said. "And the lights?"

The boy was a black shadow now that the headlights were off, weak evening light in from the open garage door useless. He believed Lawrence shrugged at the question. "I don't know," Lawrence said, then, "Promise you won't be mad."

"Mad about what?" Larry said. "About the lights?" He came around the car, stood before his son. "Mad about what?"

"Just promise," the shadow said. "It's no big deal, really. But you have to promise."

"All right," he said, and wondered what this might all be about. "I promise."

Lawrence said, "I got a tattoo."

"You *what?*" He tried to focus on the figure before him. "You got a *what?*"

"A tattoo," Lawrence said, and now he saw his son moving, turning toward him, pushing up, he believed, his T-shirt sleeve. "A couple days ago. I saved up for it." He paused, as though Larry might be able to see his arm in the dark. "I was waiting for the scab to come off before I showed it to you and Mom."

"You *what?*" Larry said again. "You're thirteen years old!"

"Dad," his son said, "you promised. You promised me you wouldn't get mad."

"Where is your mother?" he said, and brushed past his son, took the three steps up to the kitchen door, pushed it open, his son silent behind him, his moves, he knew, too quick and hard even to allow an answer. He would find her, see what she had to say about this.

The kitchen was dark, the only light the pale purple in from the windows, so that it seemed he might be walking in a dream, the things around him—the refrigerator, the breakfast nook table, the sofa and chairs in the family room, the hall table, even the individual rungs of the banister as he mounted the stairs— as pale and meaningless as the empty sky outside.

What was with these lights?

He found Debbie in their bedroom, saw her—in the instant he pushed open the door—throw something from where she stood at her dresser to something big and dark lying on their bed.

It was a suitcase, he made out, open.

"This is it," she said, "this is it, this is it."

"What are you doing?" Larry said, and came to the bed, saw

sail from the dresser to the suitcase before him a wad of some-thing. Clothing, he believed. Hers.

"This is it," she said, and slammed shut a drawer. He saw her figure bend at the waist, heard a drawer scrape open, saw more wads of clothing fly.

"Honey," he said. "Debbie," he said, "what's going on?"

She stood then, and he heard her breathing, sharp and hard in the growing dark of their bedroom.

"I'm having an affair," she said, and then it seemed she burst, those sharp and hard breaths gone in an instant, replaced with sobs as open and clear as the day had seemed when he'd backed out of the driveway this morning, as open and clear as when he'd put that red flag up to signal the mailman.

Had he known this was coming? he wondered. Were there signs? What had he missed?

He turned, sat on the edge of the bed, his back to his sob-bing wife. She sobbed, still at the dresser, and he wondered what words there were for this, for something he hadn't fore-seen.

What might he say, now that everything had been lost? And did his job even matter now, the death of a janitor and all those schoolchildren forced to hold class in camp tents donated by families in town nothing more than an odd item in the news-paper, a funny photograph he and Mr. Hemley had laughed over just yesterday morning, when the world lay before them, untainted and pure?

What about his son's tattoo?

And what was with these lights?

He looked up, saw the switch by the door, the one that controlled the ceiling fan in here, and the lights.

He'd laid out the wiring schematic on this house himself. He'd done that work, and for the last seven years had rested each night with the good knowledge he'd done his work well, all the lights working, and that ceiling fan, even the garage door opener.

But what would happen were he now to flip on the lights in here at that switch plate? Would he, too, fry as had the janitor? Would his wife sob even louder were he to die here, his own house razed by his inept schematics?

Was this how his life would end? he wondered, and believed, perhaps, it already had: His wife was having an affair, his thirteen-year-old had a tattoo, his boss had left with the softball trophy.

Why not try? he wondered.

He stood, went to the switch plate. Still Debbie sobbed, there at the dresser, and it seemed the few feet to that switch plate had suddenly become a maze a mile long, as much an ordeal as a day courting Laqueesha and Dorinda and avoiding the eyes of Benny O'Hearn, the bastard.

He reached the wall, put his hand to the switch. He swallowed, closed his eyes, and here came a picture of that janitor in the moment before he touched those wires, beside him a galvanized bucket of clouded antiseptic water, a mop in the other hand, his feet planted square in the patch of wet linoleum he'd just finished cleaning.

He opened his eyes then, blinked away that image. He'd

done a good job on the wiring here. Yet he'd believed he'd done a good job on that Burger King napkin as well. Still, the school had burned down.

And it came to him: Things happened, he only now knew, took strange twists away from you, and in a single second headed straight for hell in a handbasket with no input from you whatsoever.

That, he finally realized, was the way things worked.

He flipped up the switch.

Nothing happened.

"That's nothing," Debbie managed to say then, her voice winded, empty, relieved of itself for how openly and clearly she had sobbed. "That's nothing," she said again, and turned from the dresser, headed for the master bath. "Listen to this," she said, and he followed her, saw her in the near black of the bathroom twist at the faucets of their double sinks. Immediately the room filled with sound, rapid-fire thuds from air-filled pipes.

"No water," she said. "No water, and no electricity." She paused, and here were the sharp and hard breaths again. "I'm having an affair," she said, and the sobbing began again.

He'd had nothing to do with the plumbing in here, and for a moment felt relief, felt himself almost smile. He had nothing to do with the plumbing.

But then his life came back to him, and he lost the smile.

He turned, left her there in the bathroom, left the rapid-fire thuds and her sobbing, and went to the window across the dark room to see what this day's last moments of light might bring.

He saw out there a blue sky so dark and heavy he knew it would be only a moment or two before the black would take over completely, and stars would emerge like celestial master electricians come to jeer at him, his life out of his hands.

"Citibank called today," his wife sobbed from the bathroom. "They canceled the cards. They said they called TRW, too, and told them to put our name on their shit list." She took in several quick breaths.

He noticed then that no other lights were on in any of the houses he could see. Not in the Tolmans' across the street, or the Neezaks' to their right, the Dohertys' to their left. He saw no streetlamps, either, only darkened streets and a deep blue sky empty of stars, as though perhaps this were the end of the world, and civilization as he knew it—a garage door opener that worked, a faithful wife, the United States Postal Service picking up his mail—was finished. Done and done.

"They put a lien on the house, too," she sobbed. "The bank." She took in more quick breaths. "And Ed Hemley," she sobbed, "is great in bed."

His life, done and done.

Then, out there in this evening he believed to be on the cusp of the Apocalypse, he saw the headlights of a car down on the street, moving slowly, stopping, moving slowly again, stopping before each house a moment, as though in search of an address, and he imagined it might very well be the same officer as had served papers on Mr. Hemley—Ed, now—come to get him, and he crossed his arms, held himself, waited for whatever might come next.

It stopped next door at his neighbor's house a moment, then pulled to his own.

A white jeep, there at his mailbox.

The mailman.

He saw the mailman lean out, flip open the door on his mailbox, saw him extract small slips of paper, saw him insert some of his own. He saw all this beneath a sky as close to black as a sky might ever be, and still hold no stars, and thought it a miracle somehow, so dark out there, and yet light enough for him to see the quick flick of the mailman's wrist, a practiced move as professional and smooth and confident in itself as anything he had ever seen, and then he saw the mailman look up to him, here in this darkened window, and saw, he believed, the mailman smile up at him, saw him wink, then wave, a brief gesture filled with possibility and courage.

Larry felt his own hand move of its own accord, and he, too, waved, the same gesture a passing on of something: courage, he thought. Courage, and possibility.

And one by one, throughout his neighborhood, he saw lights come on. Here, there, the next blocks over, then the Tolmans, and the Neezaks, and the Dohertys, until his hometown seemed a spray of celestial gifts, myriad constellations, a map of the galaxy, untainted and pure. Who needed stars? he thought.

Then his own lights came on, first downstairs, and he saw that light he knew from every other night spill softly onto the sidewalk and lawn and driveway; next came upstairs, this room in which he stood with his wife, and all view of the night outside was suddenly gone, replaced by his own reflection in the glass,

the lights on behind him, so that what he saw was a man, himself, with his arm up in a kind of snappy salute, confident in
himself.

Debbie had stopped sobbing, and he turned, saw her where
he'd been on the edge of the bed. She was weeping now, carefully, gently, and he went to her, put his arm around her, held
her.

He heard water flowing now, saw from where they sat on the
bed into the bathroom clear water stream from the faucets, the
water back on.

"I was lying. I'm not having an affair," she wept. "I would
never do that to you. I just want you to cherish me," she wept.
"That's all."

He held her, held her close, watched the water flow, smelled
his wife, her hair, that same shampoo she always used, and the
phone rang.

He would not answer it, he decided, chose instead to cherish
her in this moment. But it rang only once anyway, and he held
Debbie close, smelled her hair.

Then it rang again, and though this time he thought perhaps
he ought to answer—maybe this was Ed Hemley calling, beg-
ging Larry to come bail him out—the phone again rang only
once, and no more.

"There," he whispered to Debbie. "I cherish you," he whispered, "you know I cherish you," and thought of the mailman's
wave, his own perfect copy in the glass reflection, and thought,
too, of how he might get the library bid on his own. Hemley
Electric, Inc., was ripe for a takeover, he thought. And the wir-

ing wasn't, finally, his own fault; Mr. Hemley had in fact given him the okay; no way was he liable for it. No way.

He heard a small and tentative knock on the doorjamb, and turned, saw—standing in the doorway—Lawrence, who smiled, gave a small, tentative wave. "Can I come in?" he said.

Debbie sniffed, sat up straight, dabbed at her eyes. She gave Larry a nod, a broken smile.

"Come on in," Larry said.

Lawrence took a step into the room, and another. He said, "I answered the phone." He shrugged. "The first one was somebody from Citibank." He shrugged again, smiled. "The guy said they made a mistake, and now they have you down as paid up. The guy said he was sorry and that he'd called TRW, whoever that is." He shrugged yet again, still smiled. "He said this TRW was wiping clean your life. That was what he said, 'TRW is wiping clean your life.' And they've upped your credit limit, too."

Larry looked at Debbie, whose smile was no longer broken but strong and healthy.

"Who's TRW?" Lawrence said, then, "And what's a lien? Because that was what the second one was about. Some lady from Bank of America said the lien was off, and it was a big mistake, the mortgage was in."

"When you're older," Larry said, and felt himself smile, "you'll understand about all this." He patted the bed next to him, said, "Come sit down. It's been a long day."

Lawrence came to the bed, sat beside him, his hands in his lap. He shrugged.

Still Larry smiled, smiled at this faithful wife, a loving son, lights and water. He smiled at Citibank, and the mortgage, and the miracle of the mailman, the graceful bestowal of fortune he'd signaled was on its way with a smile and wave of his hand. All this, in just the smallest of gestures.

"Can I show it to you now?" Lawrence said. "In the light?"

"What?" Larry said, his smile grown to beaming now, the way the world worked no surprise at all, finally: a representative from the United States Postal Service had arrived, taken up those obligations, and sent them on their way, the world a wonderful place, full of possibility and courage. The way things worked.

"My tattoo," Lawrence said.

"You're just kidding, right?" Larry said, still beaming.

"No," Lawrence said, his own smile grown into its own beam, and he looked to Debbie, beaming on her own. They all beamed.

Lawrence rolled up his T-shirt sleeve. He said, "I saved up for this for five months."

There at the top of his son's shoulder was a tattoo, a jagged bolt of red lightning six inches long, its edges crisp and keen, beneath it a scroll, the word *Dad* stitched into the skin of his thirteen-year-old son's arm.

It was beautiful.

"This isn't one of those wash-off kid's things, is it?" Larry asked.

"Nope," Lawrence said. "Permanent," he said, and nodded.

"Good," Larry said. "Young people these days need something they can depend on," he said, and put his free arm around him.

He held his wife, held his son, and decided he would give his son a raise in his allowance, give him a boost toward the next tattoo, one for Debbie, and imagined a heart, pink and plump, on his other shoulder, *Mom* stitched there.

Ed Hemley served with papers. That was something. And the janitor's family would come out all right after this, once they'd settled out of court.

Water flowed, light fell.

What more could he ask?

GESTURE

HE TOOK THE BOX DOWN FROM THE SHELF, FOUND ANOTHER PAIR of running shoes in it, as in every other box he'd pulled down. Eleven of them so far, and it looked in the dark of the top of the closet as though there were maybe ten or so more.

Just shoe boxes stacked on the top shelf, in every one of them a worn-down pair of running shoes, some scuffed, some still with mud in the tracks of the soles, some with broken laces, some with Velcro straps pulled apart and put together so many times they no longer held.

This was two days after the funeral, his father's death a surprise: He was sixty-four, ran four miles every day, and just Sunday evening he'd talked to Paul on the phone, asked after Kate and David and Jill. His voice had sounded fine, as predictable as ever: clear, sharp. So normal Paul had thought nothing of the conversation, merely filed it away as Dad's Sunday evening call, him alive and well and two hours north, the words passed between them forgotten as easily as hanging up the phone.

Then he'd gotten the call Monday morning, a doctor from the hospital in North Myrtle Beach. His father had died in the kitchen of cardiac arrest, just back from his morning run. He'd been able to call 911 himself, but had died before the paramedics made it over.

Now here was Paul with these shoes, this empty condominium, his sister and two brothers already headed back to their lives a variety of states away, himself and his family left to sift through, report back.

He brought down another box, opened it, saw another pair: New Balance, blue. Then he brought down the next, and the next, as though convinced somehow one of these might yield something else, some other shard of his father. Something.

But they were all only shoes.

Kate sat at the kitchen table, a stack of file folders before her. She had one open, her fingers moving through the papers, looking for what, Paul could not say. But she was working, doing something. Gathering information as though this were her job, and not simply the last evidence of her husband's father. David and Jill were at the movies, a matinee, dispatched there by Kate, David quietly gleeful even through the shroud of grief both he and his sister wore: Though they had both sobbed openly at the gravesite only day before yesterday, David was in the car before Jill had on her jacket, month-old driver's license in his wallet.

Paul stood beside Kate, and she looked up at him, tried at a smile. She picked up her coffee cup, the words LIVE TO RUN, RUN TO LIVE: SENIORS 10K wrapped around it. She said, "Some for me?"

Paul nodded, took her cup to the counter, filled it and his too: on Paul's cup a swirled painting of the bridges from Charleston to Mount Pleasant, beneath it the words COOPER RIVER BRIDGE RUN.

He looked at their two cups, the coffee inside them black, all the more black for the white insides of the cups, then opened the cupboards above the coffeemaker. There he saw what he'd seen every time he'd been here: rows and rows of coffee cups, each with a different logo or picture or slogan from six- and ten-K runs all over the South.

They were the same cups as ever. Maybe one or two or three new ones since the last time he'd been here. But they were the same.

He stood with his hands on the cupboard handles, hanging on, he felt, as though, were he to let go, he might fall away, disappear. This was about his father, all these cups.

He swallowed, said, "Look at this."

He heard Kate behind him turn in her chair. She said, "What?"

"These cups," he said, uncertain as to whether or not he'd spoken or whispered the words. He held on.

He heard her stand, moving toward him.

He let go the handles then, and nothing happened. Here he stood. He hadn't fallen, hadn't disappeared. And now he felt Kate's hand at his back, felt her lean into his shoulder.

His father had begun running a week or so after Paul's mother had died. Fifteen years ago, back when Paul and Kate still lived in California, back before Paul'd been transferred to Charleston. Back then they were at such a remove from his father's life that the running had seemed to Paul a mere hobby, something talked about on the phone, like stamp collecting or cleaning out the garage on a regular basis.

But then they had visited him in North Myrtle Beach on their way out to Charleston, had stopped in for a week. That first night they'd stayed up late, Paul wound up from the day-long drive, the tail end of a trip across the country, and they'd talked, Kate and the kids already in bed. They talked of Paul's new position with the medical supply firm, of the house he'd picked out for them in Mount Pleasant, talked too of the life his father had set up here. And they'd talked, finally, of Paul's mother, and of how much they both missed her, how much they loved her.

Then, abruptly, Paul's father stood, said he had to get to bed, that he couldn't be late getting up tomorrow morning to run with his friends. He'd given Paul a hug, and disappeared down the hall.

And Paul had thought this was nice, his father's having friends he could do something with.

Next morning he'd heard sounds from the kitchen, he and Kate in bed in the spare room. He'd gotten up, seen it was five forty-five, the sky still dark outside, and made his way down the hall toward light from the kitchen.

There sat Jill and David—they were still little then, David six, Jill four—at the kitchen table, before them bowls of cereal, his father in the middle of the kitchen, stretching.

He had on Day-Glo–orange running shorts, a white T-shirt with the stylized figure of a runner on it, all blurred blue angles and lines, in a circle around it the words RUN FOR YOUR LIFE! He had on a pair of running shoes, what looked in the light like an elaborate scheme of red and white leather pieces slung low about his feet, the soles broad and rolling high at the toe.

He was smiling at the kids, said, "Now this is to stretch the quadriceps," and he bent a leg at the knee, reached behind him, and grabbed the toe of the shoe. "You do that so when you're out there running, your body'll be ready for the work. No surprises to your body that way." Jill had giggled for some reason, kicked her legs beneath the chair, her spoon tight in her hand. She hadn't even seen Paul come in, nor had David, who only dug into his bowl of cereal—it looked like box granola, as far as Paul could see in the kitchen light—and took a mouthful, chewed.

His father had glanced up at him, nodded, still smiling, then let go his leg, bent the other leg at the knee, reached back with the other hand and pulled at the toe. "Got to bend so you won't break," he said, and nodded once more at Paul. Still Jill giggled, still David ate. Neither of them saw him, only watched their grandfather stretch.

And now Paul—standing in the same kitchen his children had eaten in that morning ten years ago, their grandfather before them in a strange outfit that bore no resemblance to anything Paul had ever seen his father wearing—he wondered why he had never asked after this hobby of his father's, why he hadn't at least inquired of him that morning who his friends were or— every Sunday-night phone call from then on—ask why, why had he started doing this: running?

Of course it would have to do with his mother, her death. He knew this, figured all these years it was something to do to fill the empty void of time his life must have then encountered, the time Paul himself knew well enough was already consumed by itself in a way that seemed in fact to deny time: here was his son, sixteen and driving already, when in only this moment he had been six years old, his daughter four, the two of them watching their grandfather in a house dark save for one light above this kitchen table, him warning them to bend so they wouldn't break.

He looked at the cup in his hands, at the white inside it. The black coffee there swirled with the slightest movement of his wrist, and he wondered what he knew of his father, what he really knew.

And things came to him.

This: His father is driving the family out to San Fernando from Buena Park Sunday afternoon to visit grandparents; to get there, they pass through the Hollywood Freeway tunnel, and each time they do Paul's father honks the horn, just a quick snap of sound in the dark that echoes a moment and disappears. Each time they pass through the tunnel, each time he honks the horn, other cars do the same in what seems some tacit code of disobedience. Each time, too, no one in the car says a word, only watches, Paul and his brothers and sister all smiling, waiting for their father to honk, then turn in his seat, smile back at them, nod as he does every time, and it is this waiting that is important to him, waiting for his father to do what they know he will do, and does. This predictable rebellion he sees in his father.

This: One evening when Paul is seven his father comes home from the newly vacant house two doors down, his right hand wrapped in the tail of his white shirt, that tail brilliant red with blood, his left hand holding it tight; with him is Mr. Murray from the end of the block, Paul's best friend Steve's dad, who'd had in mind to swap out the garage door springs from the empty house for the old rusted ones in his own. Now his father is hurt, he's trying not to cry, Paul can see in his eyes as he stands just inside the kitchen and holding that shirttail too red, Paul and his brothers and sister moving back and away from him while Mr. Murray and Mom hover around him, Paul's mother peeling back the tail to take a look, silent the whole time while Mr. Murray keeps saying *I'm sorry, I'm sorry, it's all my fault.* Paul's mother's face reveals nothing at what she sees and what Paul cannot, his mother and father and Mr. Murray then leaving for the hospital, Mrs. Murray showing up a moment later with Steve, all of them puzzled, even Mrs. Murray, as to what to do next in an empty kitchen. That is when Paul looks down at the linoleum in front of the sink, where the three adults had stood, and sees three thick drops of brilliant red, a perfect triangle of his father's blood.

And this: His father stands at the stove in the kitchen of that same house in Buena Park, poking at a pan of burning scrambled eggs, the smell a thick and ugly reminder throughout the house that their mother is in the hospital, Paul's baby sister born just the day before. But his father is here, smiling with the pan in hand and scooping up the blackened stuff onto their plates.

His father, making dinner.

He feels Kate's hand on his shoulder, the two of them side by side at this kitchen counter, and he looks a moment longer at the coffee, swirls it again with the slightest movement of his wrist, a world of movement in this small cup, and turns to his wife, meets her eyes.

She says, "It will be okay," and though he knows the words to be hollow, he knows them too to be the best ones available, the truest lie he can hear right now.

He shrugs. He thinks of the shoes, of all those coffee cups.

He thinks of his mother, and of her smiling in the smallest way each time Paul's dad honks the horn; the corners of her mouth turned up only a fraction, he'd seen there in the dark of the tunnel each time.

And he hears the instant of sound the horn makes, the echoes of others behind and around them. Small sounds, inconsequential. But there, real.

He sees his father running, and running, and begins, this moment, to understand.

He says, "How long before the kids get back?" and before Kate can answer, before she can leave his side to find this morning's newspaper, a paper delivered to the home of a man no longer alive, his father, Paul begins to line up stories to tell them of his father's life, and hopes in the same instant, though he knows it may be a chance as slight and ephemeral as an instant of sound echoed off the walls of a tunnel, that his children might have already begun forming their own stories of him.

He will make them dinner, he decides. Perhaps scrambled eggs.

It is an empty gesture, he knows. A move that will serve only as a symbol to himself: his children's father, making dinner in his own father's house.

But what more can he provide? What else is there left to do, save feed his children, and begin now to grieve?

POSTSCRIPT

IT SEEMED EACH MORNING HE WOULD NEVER FIND THE RIGHT words for the story. Things happened around him: His children came in with Lego problems, his friends called, his mother grew old, his father up and died on him, his children left the house for hours on end with the car, then came back, years later, with other children, children of their own. And still his wife called to him with chores, chores that seemed only more clutter: Take the garbage to the curb, mow the lawn, oil this door, pack those boxes, sign here on this line and drive the truck four states west, then help me with the corn, keep the silk inside the sink.

All this, while still he sat with these words swirling about him in absurd order, words lined up like drunken soldiers, like harlots with painted lips slurring just as drunkenly as those soldiers he'd thought up. But even that idea of words like harlots and soldiers lined up before him began to stink of a lie—how could words line up like drunken soldiers and harlots?—while around him now his mother died and still more children paraded through the house and his own children, the children who had had those Lego problems only this morning, came into the afternoon light of his office where still he tried to work to tell him of mortgages and insurance and tuition, all cares of a world he wanted out of in order to get these words right, get these lost and swirling words in line before him in some sort of order so that they might bow to him, might surrender to him perhaps a moon over a midnight lake, that lake flat and black and clean, the surface so smooth that next there might come a second moon just beneath the first, a moon descending into its own black sky, this lake, the higher its sister moon rose over this lake of words he wanted smoothed for him.

That was what he wanted: that moon. Both of them. Maybe even that black sky thrown in for good measure.

But nothing came to him. No moons, no midnight lakes. Eventually, too, his wife stopped calling to him and oiled doors herself, kept the silk inside the sink, kissed the children goodbye, until finally he looked up, saw outside his window a sky gone the perfect black of a midnight sky, a perfect moon rising just like a moon.

One moon, all by itself. No help from him at all.

ACKNOWLEDGMENTS

The author would like to thank the editors of the following
magazines, anthologies, and radio programs in which these
works originally appeared:

"Family" in *Prairie Schooner*

"The Difference Between Women and Men" and "A
Way Through This" on National Public Radio's
The Sound of Writing

"Somebody Else" and "An Evening on the Cusp of the
Apocalypse" in *Ascent*

"A Part of It" (in slightly different form) in *ACM* (*Another
Chicago Magazine*)

"Rose" in *Shenandoah*

"The Issue of Money" (in slightly different form) in *Gambit*

"Nostalgia" in *Hunger Mountain*

"Gesture" and "Halo" in *Arts and Letters*

"Everything Cut Will Come Back" in *The Idaho Review*

"Postscript" in *Sudden Stories: A Mammoth Anthology
of Minuscule Fiction*

"The Difference Between Women and Men" also appeared
in the anthology *Listening to Ourselves: NPR's Short Story
Magazine of the Air*

"The Train, the Lake, the Bridge" appeared in the anthologies *Ghost Writing: Haunted Tales by Contemporary Authors* and *Year's Best Horror and Fantasy Stories, 2001*

"Rose" also appeared in the anthologies *Crossroads: Southern Stories of the Fantastic* and *A Confederacy of Crime*

About the Author

BRET LOTT is the author of the novels *A Song I Knew by Heart,*
Jewel (an Oprah's Book Club selection in 1999), *Reed's Beach,*
A Stranger's House, The Man Who Owned Vermont, and *The*
Hunt Club; the story collections *A Dream of Old Leaves* and *How*
to Get Home; the memoir *Fathers, Sons, and Brothers;* and a book
of his essays on writing, *Before We Get Started.* He and his
wife live in Baton Rouge, Louisiana, where he is editor of *The*
Southern Review and professor of English at Louisiana State
University.

About the Type

This book is set in Fournier, a typeface named for Pierre Simon Fournier, the youngest son of a French printing family. Pierre Simon first studied watercolor painting, but became involved in type design through work that he did for his eldest brother. Starting with engraving woodblocks and large capitals, he later moved on to fonts of type. In 1736 he began his own foundry, and published the first version of his point system the following year. He made several important contributions in the field of type design; he cut and founded all the types himself, pioneered the concepts of the type family, and is said to have cut sixty thousand punches for 147 alphabets of his own design. He also created new printers' ornaments.

Pierre Simon Fournier is probably best remembered as the designer of St. Augustine Ordinaire, one of the early transitional faces. It served as the model for the Monotype transitional face Fournier, which was released in 1925.